THE SEA KING

SIR FRANCIS DRAKE AND HIS TIMES

THE SEA KING

SIR FRANCIS DRAKE AND HIS TIMES

Albert Marrin

ATHENEUM BOOKS FOR YOUNG READERS

Atheneum Books for Young Readers
An imprint of Simon & Schuster
1230 Avenue of the Americas
New York, New York 10020

Book design by Anne Scatto / PIXEL PRESS
Maps on pages 38, 56-57, 116 copyright © by Virginia Norey

The text of this book is set in Monotype Columbus

First edition

Printed in the United States of America

10 9 8 7 6 5 4 3 2 1

Library of Congress Catalog Card Number: 95-060386

And bold and hardened adventures to undertake
Leaving his country for his country's sake.
　　　　　—Charles Fitzgeoffrey, *Sir Francis Drake,* 1596

Contents

THE SEA KING

SIR FRANCIS DRAKE AND HIS TIMES

SIR FRANCIS DRAKE AS HE LOOKED AT THE HEIGHT OF HIS
FAME AND FORTUNE.

A Self-Made Man

*D*eptford, England, April 4, 1581. A glorious spring day with high fleecy clouds and a light breeze blowing across the Thames River. Dawn had not yet broken when crowds began to gather along the riverbank, the dozens of tiny river craft crowded with sightseers bobbed in the gentle swells. It was a festival day, a day of rejoicing, and no one wanted to miss a minute of it.

All eyes were fixed on the ship anchored close to shore. A small, handy vessel, she glistened in the morning sun. And well she might, since sailors had been rubbing and scrubbing and polishing as if their lives depended upon it. St. George's flag, the national flag, a giant red cross on a white field, fluttered at the top of her mainmast. The royal banners hung from her other masts, each with its red and gold lions and blue and gold lilies.

Known as the *Golden Hind*, the ship had recently returned after an absence of nearly three years. It had been a fantastic adventure. She had made the longest voyage in history and was the first English vessel to sail around the world. In doing so, her captain and crew had not only stored up memories to last a lifetime, but also a vast treasure stolen from the Spanish colonies on the western coast of South America.

Spain's ambassador to England did not try to hide his rage with polite diplomatic language. The captain, he hissed, was "the master thief of the unknown world." As a pirate, he deserved nothing more (or less) than a fast trial and a faster execution, preferably a painful one. Yet "these English" had come to admire the pirate ship and idolize its captain. What a people!

As the hours passed, the excitement grew both ashore and aboard the *Golden Hind*. Toward noon, the guest of honor arrived. She came in a magnificent coach, announced by blaring trumpets and galloping horsemen. Her subjects cheered when she came in view. They called her Gloriana, Good Queen Bess, and the Virgin Queen, because she never married. History knows her as Elizabeth I, England's greatest queen. The years of her reign, 1558–1603, are known as the Elizabethan Age.

A narrow bridge had been built from the shore to the ship's deck. Elizabeth began to walk across, when one of her purple and gold garters slipped off. A member of the royal party picked it up, begging to keep it as a souvenir. She smiled, saying she had nothing else with which to keep her stocking up. Then, for all to see, she hiked up her gown and slid the garter up to her knee.

Stepping aboard the *Golden Hind*, she found its captain kneeling before her on one knee, his hat in his hand. Francis Drake was a striking figure. A man of about thirty-six, he was short, heavyset, and looked as if he was used to hard physical work outdoors. From his broad chest to his sturdy limbs, he radiated power and self-confidence. He had a ruddy complexion, brown hair, a beard of the same color cut to a point, and a moustache with the tips twirled upward. His eyes were deep gray, large, round, and clear; there was a red scar under his right eye, caused by the arrow of a South American Indian. A complicated person, his character was like a diamond with many facets. He was boastful, vain, arrogant, hot-tempered, ambitious, and loved flattery. Yet he was also smart, brave, loyal, patriotic, and god-fearing. No captain treated his crew with more consideration than he; even captives praised his courtesy and generosity. He never shed blood unless absolutely necessary.

Elizabeth motioned for him to rise and, resting her hand on his arm, asked him to show her around the *Golden Hind*. Drake led her from stem to stern, from the quarterdeck above to the gun deck below. The tour ended on the main deck, where an elegant banquet had been set.

After the banquet, Her Majesty ordered her host to kneel once again. "Master Drake," she said solemnly, a slight frown on her face. "The King of Spain has asked for your head, and we have a weapon here with which to remove it."

One of the court gentlemen gave her a gilded sword, which she handed to a visiting French nobleman. "We shall ask Monsieur . . . to be the headsman."

No one quite knew what to expect until it happened. The Frenchman stepped forward and tapped Drake's right shoulder with the flat of the blade. As he did so, the queen's voice rang out for all to hear: "Arise, Sir Francis Drake!" Instead of beheading him, she had made him a knight, turning a commoner into a nobleman. Drake showed his gratitude by giving her a small memento of the occasion: a golden frog encrusted with diamonds. It was considered good manners, whenever the queen paid a visit, for the host to give her a valuable gift as a token of respect. No one would have dreamed of doing otherwise.

A coat of arms went along with the title. Like all coats of arms, Drake's told a story and taught a lesson in symbols and words. It showed a ship balanced on top of a globe; below was the Latin motto *Sic Parvis Magna*—"Greatness from small beginnings." That was a perfect description of the man and his achievements.

Sir Francis Drake is England's most famous seaman. From start to finish, his life was an adventure the likes of which few have ever experienced. Truly a "self-made man," he was the poor boy who made good. Rising from humble beginnings, he became a legend not only in his own time, but for all time. Though the English had always been a seafaring people, they had never accomplished anything of real importance at sea. Other peoples found the New World and opened trade with the Far East. By showing that an Englishman could sail anywhere, Drake gave his countrymen the confidence to go out and win an empire.

More, he showed that a small country could stand up to a superpower if it had the will and the know-how. Sixteenth-century England opposed the Spanish Empire, which threatened the independence of all West European nations. Rich and powerful, its armies the finest in Europe, Spain seemed invincible. Drake, however, proved that the enemy was vulnerable, that it could be attacked, plundered, humiliated. By doing so, he filled his people with pride, encouraged Spain's foes, and weakened Spanish morale. He and his cousin John Hawkins also taught their countrymen how to fight at sea. Thanks to them, Britannia ruled the waves for nearly three centuries. They created the warship—sleek, fast, heavily gunned—that would dominate the Age of Fighting Sail.

The name of Sir Francis Drake will be honored as long as free people go down to the sea in ships.

CHAPTER I

Young Mariner

May you live in interesting times.
—AN ANCIENT CHINESE CURSE

Francis Drake's early life is largely a mystery. He was born sometime between 1540 and 1545 on a farm near Tavistock in Devon, a county in southwestern England. Neighbors said that his father, Edmund, had been a sailor before settling down and marrying a woman whose name has been lost to history. Nothing is known about her except that she bore him twelve sons, of whom Francis was the first—or the first to survive, since disease claimed half of all sixteenth-century children before their first birthday.

Francis was born into a world in turmoil, a world divided into warring camps. When his father was a boy, a German monk named Martin Luther began the Protestant Reformation. Luther denounced the Roman Catholic church as corrupt and worldly. The church, he insisted, had rejected the simple virtues of Christianity for the sake of wealth, power, and luxury. In protesting, he demanded reform, in short, a Protestant Reformation.

Luther's ideas landed like a bombshell. Until he came along, Europeans had been bound together by a common faith and outlook. Nations might disagree, even fight, but they still shared the same religious and moral beliefs. The spread of the Reformation, however, forced people to choose sides. Europe at that time knew nothing of religious liberty or the separation of church and state. Faith and citizenship went hand in hand. To be a good citizen, not only did you have to

MARTIN LUTHER, A
GERMAN MONK, BEGAN
THE PROTESTANT
REFORMATION BY
BREAKING WITH THE
ROMAN CATHOLIC
CHURCH IN THE 1520S.
BEFORE LONG,
PROTESTANTS AND
CATHOLICS WERE
PERSECUTING EACH
OTHER AND FIGHTING
RELIGIOUS WARS
THROUGHOUT WESTERN
EUROPE.

obey the law, you had to follow the "true religion," that is, the religion of your ruler.

Rulers used their power to keep their people loyal to Catholicism or to lead them into the Protestant camp. Those who objected were deemed worse than traitors; they were heretics, teachers of false beliefs, who belonged in hell. Heretics were persecuted, often killed, to keep them from "killing" the souls of innocent people. Thus began a cycle of violence lasting two centuries. Persecuted minorities resisted whenever possible, plunging one country after another into revolution or civil war. Wars between nations became crusades. In addition to their usual quarrels over trade and territory, nations claimed to be fighting for God, truth, and holiness. The Reformation, therefore, was far more than a religious movement. Much of what follows in this book could not have happened without it.

In England King Henry VIII and his son, Edward VI, broke with the Catholic church in the 1530s and 1540s. That was fine with Edmund Drake, an ardent Protestant. Many of his neighbors, however, still clung to the old faith. In 1549 Catholic mobs went on a rampage in Devon, forcing the Drakes to abandon their farm. They fled eastward, settling near the main base of the Royal Navy at the mouth of the Thames. Edmund supported his family by reading the Bible and preaching to the ships' crews. It was a poorly paid occupation, and the family had to make its home on a mastless, rotten hulk anchored offshore.

Years later, after Francis had become famous, he admitted, "My bringing up hath not been in learning."[1] Whatever he knew of reading and writing had been learned at his father's knee. Nevertheless, he had a natural ability with words. He spoke passionately and convincingly, so that even doubters came around to his way of thinking.

Edmund gave his son his outlook on the world. He taught him that God is master of all things, and that whatever happens, good or bad, is according to a divine plan. Francis learned to accept any failure as due to God's will, although, he confessed, it might be difficult to understand. He had no trouble, however, understanding that Catholics were wicked. From his earliest days, he disliked Catholics. Like his father, he called them "idolaters," "enemies of God," and "papists," that is, servants of the pope in Rome. Dislike turned to hatred after Queen Mary came to the English throne in 1553. Known as Bloody Mary, she was a fanatic Catholic. Determined to undo the work of her father and brother, she sent hundreds of Protestants to the executioner. After her death in 1558 her Protestant half-sister, Elizabeth, took over and ruled forty-five years.

Young Drake, however, had still another teacher: the sea. Life at the edge of the sea was different from anything he had known on the farm. There were different sights, different smells, and different sounds along the shore. Fields and trees gave way to a forest of tall masts. Wherever he turned he saw white sails, anchors, and guns—lots of guns. The air was heavy with the smell of salt, tar, and damp wood. The whistling of the wind mingled with the sounds of creaking timbers and gurgling water as his home rose and fell with the tides.

Since the family was large and the father's income small, the eldest

RELIGIOUS PERSECUTION IN ENGLAND. THE CATHOLIC QUEEN MARY, KNOWN ALSO AS "BLOODY MARY," HAD SCORES OF PROTESTANT "HERETICS," OR FALSE BELIEVERS, BURNED TO DEATH DURING HER REIGN, FROM 1553 TO 1558.

son had to go out on his own. When Francis turned ten, Edmund found him a job on a small vessel that traded with England, France, and Holland. This was not unusual; in those days boys normally went to sea at the age of ten. The life span was shorter than it is today, forcing youngsters to grow up faster. For example, boys of eight went to the wars with their fathers and girls sometimes married at nine.

The North Sea became Francis's new teacher. It was a harsh, unforgiving teacher who punished failure with death. To survive, Francis learned to navigate by the stars and compass, avoid sandbanks, and steer clear of rocky coastlines. Though only a boy, he was expected to do a man's work. This meant lending a hand when it came to hauling up the anchor, or climbing aloft to take in or unfurl the sails. It meant going sleepless for days, while storms tossed the vessel like a cork and waves swept over the deck. Yet he met every challenge; indeed, it seemed that he had been cut out for a life at sea. He became such a good sailor that his employer, a childless bachelor, remembered him in his will. And so, at about the age of sixteen, he became skipper of his own vessel.

Voyage followed voyage. Francis worked hard, spent little, and was able to put aside "a pretty sum of money." When he had enough, he decided to seek his fortune. He sold the ship and went to Plymouth, a bustling seaport in Devon. There he joined John Hawkins, a distant cousin and the town's leading citizen. Next to his father, Hawkins was to become the most important man in the youngster's life. Hawkins, who was about ten years older, had grown rich by trading with the Spanish colonies in the New World. We must leave them for a moment to take a closer look at those colonies.

*I*n the century before Drake's birth, the countries of the Iberian Peninsula—Spain and Portugal—had pioneered in overseas exploration. Between 1440 and 1520 the Portuguese explored the western coast of Africa and sailed eastward across the Indian Ocean to India, China, Japan and the East Indies, or Spice Islands. Their boldness paid off—big. Every year large ships known as carracks arrived at Lisbon, Portugal's capital and leading seaport, laden with spices, silks, and jewels. Meantime, Spain tried to find a shorter route to Asia by sailing westward. Instead, Christopher Columbus stumbled upon a new world in 1492 and Vasco Núñez de Balboa found a new ocean in 1511.

Eight years later, Ferdinand Magellan, a Portuguese working for Spain, explored that ocean, naming it the Pacific. Magellan died on the voyage, but his crew became the first to sail around the world, returning to Spain in 1522. Of the 237 men who began the voyage, only seventeen survived. Circumnavigation was a very costly business.

Both countries claimed the new lands, plus any yet to be discovered, for themselves. This was only right, they argued, since their explorers had led the way and taken all the risks. In 1494, they persuaded the pope to divide the world by an imaginary north-south line, as if it was his to divide. Everything west of the line, apart from Brazil, went to Spain; everything to the east went to Portugal. His Holiness forbade foreigners from visiting or trading with the new lands without their owners' permission. It seemed like a good deal, except that no one knew that Spain would get the best of it.

Spaniards said they came to the New World for "gold, glory, and the Gospel." True, they wished to spread the word of God and win glory by doing so. But gold came first. "Gold," Columbus wrote after his first voyage, "is the metal most excellent and above all others . . . and he who has it makes and accomplishes whatever he wishes in the world and finally uses it to send souls into Paradise."[2] Eighty years later, his words were echoed by Lope de Vega, Spain's leading playwright. In his play *The New World*, he has the devil say of his countrymen: "It is not Christianity that leads them on, but rather gold and greed." *Oro*, or "gold": The word itself seemed to drive Spaniards out of their minds. Indians called it "the crazy-making metal."

The native Americans were no match for the Spanish conquistadors. Brave warriors, they fought on foot with spears, clubs, and bows and arrows. The Spaniards had steel armor, swords, and guns. Most of all, they had horses, which did not exist in the New World until brought from Europe. Thus, no matter how outnumbered they might be, Spaniards easily won most battles. Within a generation of Columbus's arrival, they had conquered the islands of the Caribbean and founded colonies on the east coast of South America. Between 1518 and 1522 Hernan Cortés destroyed the Aztec Empire in Mexico, renaming it New Spain. In 1531 Francisco Pizarro invaded Peru with fewer than two hundred men and fifty horses. In less than five years he destroyed the Inca Empire, among the most civilized communities on earth. Both Cortés and Pizarro had been nobodies in their homeland. Now they ruled entire nations.

Mexico and Peru were a bonanza. Over the centuries, their peoples had accumulated vast amounts of gold and silver, which were promptly looted and sent to Spain. These treasures, magnificent works of art, were melted down and minted into coins.

Soon after the conquests, explorers found vast deposits of silver in both countries. Mining operations began which, before long, made the loot seem small in comparison. One-fifth of this wealth automatically went to Philip II, the Spanish king. Philip used it to pay for his armies, which in turn made him the most powerful ruler in Europe. It also allowed him to lead the Counter-Reformation, the movement to destroy Protestantism.

The colonies, however, became a magnet for Spain's enemies. The French came first. Men like Pié de Palo (Peg-Leg), Bras de Fer (Iron Arms), and Jacques de Sores struck swiftly and without mercy. Santiago de Cuba was looted, Havana burned, and Hispaniola (shared today by Haiti and the Dominican Republic) raided by a powerful force. Townspeople along the Spanish Main—the mainland of South America stretching along the coast from Venezuela to Panama—shuddered at rumors of their approach.

Colonists were also victimized by their own government. Spanish merchants, not to mention foreigners, could not sail to the New World on their own. Every ship bound for America had to join a convoy that left Spain several times a year and was guarded by warships. All trade goods had to be Spanish-made or have a royal license and be taxed by the king's treasury. These rules kept manufactured goods in short supply, and costing many times what they did at home. No wonder settlers were eager to trade with anyone clever enough to evade the law and sell at "fair" prices. They were particularly interested in buying slaves.

The Spanish colonies had a severe labor shortage. There were never enough white men to do all the necessary work, and the hot, damp climate soon wore them out if they tried. Besides, they had come to America to escape what they called *el deshonor de trabajo*, the "dishonor of work." Settlers wanted to be fine gentlemen, and gentlemen did not soil their hands.

As soon as a colony was established, the native peoples were enslaved. But the Indians made poor slaves. European diseases killed them by the millions; other millions died of overwork, starvation, or were murdered. In Hispaniola, for example, the native population fell

THE SPANISH CONQUISTADORES, OR CONQUERORS OF THE NEW WORLD, WERE CRUEL, GREEDY MEN WHO WORSHIPED GOLD. THIS PICTURE SHOWS INCA INDIANS BEING FORCED TO BRING TREASURE TO THE INVADERS DURING FRANCISCO PIZARRO'S CONQUEST OF PERU IN THE 1530s.

from more than two million in 1492 to 28,000 in little more than twenty years; in another twenty years, all were gone.

The Spanish followed a deliberate policy of terrorism, that is, using fear as a weapon, largely against the defenseless, to get their way. Bartholomé de las Casas, the first priest ordained in the New World, was ashamed of his fellow countrymen. In his *The Devastation of the Indies: A Brief Account*, a book printed in 1552, he describes the cruelties he saw with his own eyes or learned of from eyewitnesses. Indians were split in two with swords, burned alive, or drowned in batches. Runaways were tracked down and tortured to death to teach their families obedience. Anyone who displeased his master might be "dogged," that is, thrown to packs of savage hunting dogs. The priest explained:

> It is doubtful that anyone, whether Christian or not, has ever before heard of such a thing as this. The Spaniards keep alive their dogs' appetite for human beings in this way. They have Indians brought to them in chains, then unleash the dogs. The Indians come meekly down the roads and are killed. And the Spaniards have butcher shops where the corpses of Indians are hung up, on display, and someone will come in and say, more or less, "Give me a quarter of that rascal hanging there, to feed my dogs until I can kill another one for them." As if buying a quarter of a hog or other meat. Other Spaniards go hunting with their dogs in the mornings and when one of them returns at noon and is asked "Did you have good hunting?" he will reply, "Very good! I killed fifteen or twenty rascals and left them with my dogs."[3]

To save the Indians from extermination, las Casas suggested a "medicine" as awful as the sickness he hoped to cure. He suggested that the Spaniards substitute Negro for Indian labor in the mines and plantations of the New World. Only later did he realize with shame what he was asking. But by then the damage had been done and the slave trade to the New World was in full swing. It would go on for more than three centuries.

We regard slavery as a cruel, dirty business. To sixteenth-century Europeans, however, the idea of owning another person seemed perfectly natural. It had nothing to do with racism, the idea that some people are inferior and therefore "born to be slaves." Anyone might be enslaved if they were unlucky enough to be in the wrong place at the wrong time; it was simply one of life's risks, as automobile accidents are today. Muslim pirates from North Africa preyed upon Christian vessels in the Mediterranean Sea. The weak were thrown overboard; the strong were sold in Arab slave markets or chained to the oars of galleys, long, sleek warships known for their speed in calm waters. Every year Muslims kidnapped hundreds of men, women, and children from seacoast towns in Spain, France, and Italy. By the same token, the "Most Catholic King" of Spain and the "Most Christian King" of France had Muslim slaves in their galleys; indeed, Spaniards convicted of certain crimes went to the galleys for life.

Nor was African slavery new when Columbus left on his first voyage. For centuries, black Africans had been stolen by Arabs for sale in Cairo, Damascus, and Baghdad. As early as 976, an Arab ambassador caused a sensation by appearing at the court of the emperor of China

with a black slave. Portugal's Prince Henry the Navigator, a supporter of African exploration, imported the first black Africans for use as farm laborers in 1441. His people were overjoyed when some converted to Christianity—so much so that Africans were allowed to marry Portuguese. Nine years later, the pope allowed the enslavement of Africans to save their souls.

Each year dozens of ships left Lisbon for West Africa. Their destination was the "Slave Coast," the coast from Cape Verde to Sierra Leone. Sailors called this area "the white man's grave," because of the tropical diseases against which they had no immunity. Whites seldom ventured into the interior in search of slaves. Once they left their ships, they were marked men; they had to do their business quickly and put to sea before disease took hold aboard ship. Thus, the slave trade would have been all but impossible without the help of Africans themselves. Tribal chiefs were constantly at war. When prisoners were taken, chiefs either killed them on the spot or kept them as slaves. In return for knives, hatchets and colorful cloth, they gladly gave their captives to Portuguese traders. They, in turn, encouraged the chiefs to fight more wars.

Portuguese control of the Slave Coast gave them a monopoly on selling "black ivory," as the black Africans were called, in the Spanish colonies. Provided they paid a tax to the royal treasury and a commission to Philip II, they could sell up to ten thousand slaves a year. This kept the price of slaves so high that there were never enough to satisfy the demand. It was the perfect opening for a bold, enterprising man.

WEST AFRICAN TRIBESMEN PORTRAYED IN A SIXTEENTH-CENTURY DRAWING. EUROPEANS ENCOURAGED THE COASTAL TRIBES TO FIGHT EACH OTHER AND SELL THEM THEIR CAPTIVES TO BE ENSLAVED IN THE NEW WORLD.

John Hawkins became the founder of the English slave trade. At first glance, he did not seem to be cut out for such a brutal business. A good family man, he was loyal, generous, and kind. Yet these qualities did not prevent him from dealing in human misery. Misery was a part of sixteenth-century life. Conveniences that make life pleasant today were unknown. There were no air conditioners, no refrigerators, no painkilling drugs. People were accustomed to physical suffering and learned to accept it without complaint. This made them at once tough and cruel. Public executions doubled as public spectacles. Crowds enjoyed watching criminals get their just punishment, and the bloodier the better. Poisoners, for example, were plunged into boiling water or molten lead. Traitors had their bellies slit open and their guts torn out while still alive; their severed heads were then stuck on spikes set up on the stone gates at either end of London Bridge. The heads remained there, often dozens at a time, grinning at passersby until they rotted away.

To people raised in such a harsh world, the slave trade did not seem immoral. It was just good business; Hawkins referred to his cargo as "our Negroes and our other merchandise."[4] A successful slaving voyage was not cause for shame, but a sign of God's favor. Hawkins was proud of his success, taking as his insignia the image of a naked black man sitting with his hands tied. We do not know what his cousin Francis thought about this. The subject was never mentioned in his letters or in reports of his conversations.

Hawkins made two successful slaving voyages. In 1562 and 1564 he stopped Portuguese slave ships off the African coast. As their captains stared into the mouths of his cannon, he made them an offer they dared not refuse: sell him their cargoes at a good price—or else. Having collected enough "merchandise," he sailed for the Spanish Main.

Hawkins knew he was breaking Spanish law and that things would go hard for anyone who bought slaves from him. Not to worry. Upon arriving at a coastal town, he sent a message to the *alcalde* (mayor). Politely he explained that he had slaves for sale. The *alcalde*, as King Philip's loyal servant, did his duty; he denounced the intruders, threatening to open fire if they did not leave at once. This was just what Hawkins expected him to say. Immediately, boatloads of scowling sailors rowed to shore. The Spaniards met them in battle formation, each man armed to the teeth.

The Spaniards gave their battle cry: *"Santiago y a ellos!"*—"Saint James and at them!"

"Saint George for England!" the sailors shouted in return.

Flags waved. Drums beat. Guns roared.

It was very frightening, but no one was hurt; no one was *supposed* to be hurt. The "battle" was an act meant to give the settlers a cover story when the time came to explain to the king's officers. Having been defeated, they could say they had been forced to do business at gunpoint. Everybody came out ahead. Hawkins left with more gold and silver coins for the locked chest in his cabin. The settlers had the slaves they needed at a price they could afford. And the *alcalde* was satisfied because Hawkins gave him a letter praising his courage and devotion to his king.

The third voyage was to be Hawkins's most ambitious. He planned carefully, gathering at Plymouth six ships and four hundred seamen. The four smallest vessels were his own, among them the *Judith* of fifty tons,[5] commanded by Francis Drake. The largest vessels—the *Jesus* of seven hundred tons and the *Minion* of three hundred—were heavily armed and belonged to the queen, his silent partner. The Royal Navy was Her Majesty's personal property. Since she always needed money, and since her ships were not always needed for national defense, she lent them to merchants in return for a share of the profits.

The fleet sailed on October 2, 1567. The ships were "brave"—colorful—as they weighed anchor. Their hulls were painted in contrasting colors: red and white, green and white, yellow and blue. Colored cloths hung from the rigging. Bright streamers, long enough to touch the water in a dead calm, fluttered at the mastheads.

SIR JOHN HAWKINS AS SEEN BY THE PAINTER HIERONYMOUS CUSTODIS. DRAKE'S COUSIN WAS NOT ONLY A WEALTHY PLYMOUTH MERCHANT, BUT A LEADING SLAVE TRADER AND THE HEAD OF THE ROYAL DOCKYARDS, WHERE HE BUILT THE FINEST WARSHIPS OF THE TIME.

At Hawkins's signal, drums rolled and trumpets blared. Instantly, sailors sprang into action. All were barefooted and wore similar outfits: canvas breeches, linen shirts, and tight-fitting jackets called doublets.

Some of the sailors strained at the bars of heavy wooden wheels, making ropes creak against wood as anchors rose dripping mud from the harbor bottom. Others scurried up rope ladders to the yardarms, the crosspieces of the masts from which the sails hung. Suddenly there was the rustle of canvas, followed by a sharp *crack* as the sails caught the wind.

The wind breathed life into the wooden hulls. They moved, dipping and rolling and tossing spray as they headed for open water. From the shore came the clang of church bells bidding them safe journey. The

JOHN HAWKINS'S FLAGSHIP, THE JESUS, HAD A STRANGE NAME FOR A VESSEL THAT CARRIED HUMAN CARGO FOR SALE IN THE SLAVE MARKETS OF THE CARIBBEAN AND SOUTH AMERICA.

wind picked up once they slipped into the English Channel. It whistled in the shrouds, the ropes that kept the masts steady. One hour. Two hours. The shore grew dimmer as the fleet made headway. Finally, the sailors saw Lizard Point, the last corner of home, fade away on their right, or starboard. The mighty Atlantic stretched before them, vast, empty, lonely.

*T*he sailors settled into their routines. Judging from the work the men did and the dimensions of the ship, we can surmise that these men were all of a certain physical type: short, thin, wiry. Sailors had to be rather small, since a heavyweight could not go aloft on a flimsy rope ladder or balance on a slender yardarm in a stiff breeze. Similarly, a tall man would have found it difficult to move around below decks. The height between decks was 5 feet 6 inches at most; the height of the great cabin, the captain's quarters at the rear of the ship, was about 6 feet.

Everyone had his own special task. The captain commanded the vessel and was responsible for everything that happened aboard. Directly under him were the master, or navigating officer, and the quartermaster, who steered the ship. The master was also in charge of the compass, which told direction, and the astrolabe, a device for calculating the ship's position in relation to the sun or stars.

Experts at certain trades kept the ship in good working order. Among these was the boatswain, who had charge of sails, anchors, and rigging, and the chief gunner, who looked after the weapons, particularly the cannons. The sailmaker patched and mended the sails. The carpenter repaired the masts, decks, and hull. The caulker's job was to keep the ship watertight; he serviced the pumps and filled (caulked) the spaces between the timbers with a mixture of horsehair and tar. The cooper looked after the barrels in which the water and provisions were kept.

A MAN WEARING THE TYPICAL SAILOR'S COSTUME DURING THE TIME OF SIR FRANCIS DRAKE. THE COSTUME IS VERY FORMAL, WORN ONLY ON SPECIAL OCCASIONS. NORMALLY, SAILORS WORE OLD, TORN CLOTHES AND WENT ABOUT BAREFOOT.

The swabbers were forever scrubbing the oak decks and washing them down with buckets of sea water. Cleanliness had little to do with this job; the decks had to be kept moist, otherwise the planks would dry out and shrink, causing cracks to develop. The liar did the really dirty work, like collecting the garbage. "The liar," an old book on sea lore explains, "holds his place for but a week; and he that is first taken with a lie on Monday morning is proclaimed at the mainmast with a general cry, 'A liar, a liar, a liar' and for that week he is under the swabber."[6]

The captain and his officers were privileged—they slept in bunks and had private cabins. The common seaman had no place to call his own. At night he found a space on the rough lower decks, lay down, and slept as best he could. In calm, warm weather, sailors slept on deck and under the stars. Seldom did a seaman sleep soundly or for more than brief periods. Creaking timbers and rattling pumps woke him constantly. The sound of scuffling feet came from overhead, as the night watch made its rounds. At the best of times, sleeping areas were dark and stuffy, smelling of dampness and dirt. In rough weather, when the hatches were closed, life below decks was hell even for veteran seamen.

Hawkins taught his cousin to rule a ship with an iron hand. His order, read to the crews three times a week, was short and sweet: "Serve God daily, love one another, preserve your victuals, beware of fire, and keep good company." That order, albeit phrased in different ways by different captains, was the basis of discipline aboard all Elizabethan vessels. It made sense, every part of it being the result of long experience at sea.

God belonged at the head of the list. Nowhere was His power felt more keenly than at sea. He made the winds blow in the right direction, or held them back, becalming a vessel and holding it motionless until the crew died of hunger and thirst. He ruled the storms that smashed ships to splinters, and fogs that lured them onto reefs. Small wonder that prayer was said twice daily, in the morning and evening. Small wonder, too, that absence from prayer was a serious offense. It was a sign of disrespect for the Almighty, sure to bring punishment to the entire crew. For this reason the guilty party was chained alone in a dark, smelly place for twenty-four hours. Those who offended the Lord with bad language had a heavy iron spike "clapt cloese into their mouth and tyd behind their heads . . . till their mouths are very bloody."[7] Drake was so keen on religious instruction that he often preached sermons to his crews.

Failure to "love" your shipmate, that is, to treat him fairly, brought you before the captain. It was not a meeting you looked forward to. He was king of the ship. There was no protesting his rules, no appealing his decisions. His word was law, and he held the power of life and death in his hands.

The more serious the crime, the harsher the punishment. Thieves, for example, had their heads shaved and plastered with boiling tar. Anyone who drew a knife on an officer had his right hand chopped off. If you hit an ordinary sailor and drew blood, you were hoisted to the top of the highest yardarm with a rope around your waist, dropped into the sea, and pulled up again—three times. A sailor who fell asleep on watch had four chances to mend his ways. The first time he was made to stand with a bucket of water balanced on his head. The second time his arms were tied above his head and water poured into his sleeves. The third time he was tied to the mast with weights attached to his arms and legs. The fourth time, says an old document, "he shall be hang'd on the Bowsprit's end of the Ship in a basket, with a Can of Beer and a loaf of Bread and a sharp knife: choose him to hang there till he starve or cut himself into the Sea."[8] A murderer was never given a second chance. He was tied tightly to his victim, face to face, chest to chest, and thrown overboard.

Preserving victuals—saving food—was essential on a long voyage. Even so, sailors' food was barely enough, and what they had was unappetizing. The diet consisted of meat, fish, biscuit, and cheese. Meat and fish were preserved in barrels filled with salt. A barrel of meat, however, often contained an equal amount of bones and fat; the meat itself was tough and stringy. Biscuit, a type of cracker baked hard as rock, swarmed with crawling, squirming creatures, as did cheese, which was just as hard. A wise man tapped his biscuit and cheese before eating, to shake loose at least the largest tenants. "A sailor's stomach," the saying went, "could near digest iron." It had to if he expected to survive.

Meals were washed down with water or beer. Water was used not only for drinking, but for soaking the salt out of meat and fish to make them edible. Beer, however, was the favorite beverage. The English loved their brew. Everyone drank, even young children. On average, Queen Elizabeth's court consumed six hundred thousand gallons a year; sailors were allowed a gallon a day. Drunkenness was a common shipboard offense, punishable by a whipping on the bare back.

Fire prevention was a serious matter. A sailing ship was a floating firetrap. Wood, tar, rope, canvas, and paint were highly flammable. Once fire took hold, the vessel could burn down to the water in minutes. Worse, if fire came near the magazine, or gunpowder room, the ship would be blown sky-high. Anyone not burned to death almost certainly drowned; most sixteenth-century sailors could not swim. Drake could, and it saved his life at least once.

Every precaution was taken to avoid fire. Tobacco smoking was banned below decks. At night, the cook's stove was extinguished, along with all candles except those in the officers' cabins, and these were set in the middle of a saucer filled with water. Fire-fighting methods were simple, to say the least. The standard method was to chain two barrels to the sides of the ship for "the . . . mariners to piss into [so] that they may always be full of urine to quench fire with, and two or three pieces of old sail ready to wet in the piss."[9]

Hawkins's orders were silent about sanitation. There was little he could say. It was impossible to keep either the crew or the ship clean. The toilet was merely a "necessary seat," a wooden plank with holes cut in it, built out over the water in the bow. You had to be an acrobat to use this contraption even at the best of times. With the wind blowing and waves slapping, you hung on while doing your business; toilet "paper" was the end of a tarred rope, shared by everyone. Sailors were forbidden to take off their clothes during a voyage. Water was too precious to be used for washing, and there was no such thing as soap. The only people who "washed" their hands were the swabbers. Sixteenth-century Europeans had not made the connection between dirty hands and disease. Ashore, even the "best people" went years without washing their hands. The queen of Sweden, for example, claimed she didn't know the real color of her hands, having never washed them.

The officers stank. The crew stank. The ship stank. Rats, mice, and cockroaches multiplied in the dank holds. Everyone's clothes, hair, and bodies crawled with lice. Sooner or later, disease broke out. The most common shipboard diseases were bubonic plague, typhus fever, and food poisoning. The all-time killer, however, was scurvy. This disease is caused by a lack of vitamin C, found in fresh fruits and vegetables. After a few weeks at sea, men's teeth began to fall out and dark blotches appeared on the skin. They tired easily and, in time, died. Not for another century would people realize that lime juice prevented scurvy; British seamen are still called "limeys."

A ship's surgeon could set broken bones, but when it came to fighting disease, he was helpless. To begin with, he did not know how the human body worked. For example, no one knew that the heart pumped blood or why. Before the invention of the microscope, no one knew about germs, much less that they cause disease. At best, the surgeon could make his patients comfortable; at worst, he killed them. Make no mistake about it: sixteenth-century medicine was as deadly as any battle. The surgeon's favorite remedies were drawing blood to let out harmful "vapors" and giving drugs to cause vomiting; patients might be forced to vomit fifteen times a day. The medicines prescribed were disgusting. A typical prescription contained the following: sponge, cinnamon, cedarwood, red sandalwood, ivory shavings, crocus, vinegar, ground deer's heart, beetles, crushed pearls, emeralds and red coral, gold dust, and sugar. To prevent sore throats, physicians recommended sucking on dried toads. Some believed tobacco cured cancer!

*T*he crews grew restless as they neared their destination. Africa was still the "Dark Continent," a place of mystery to Europeans. Any story about Africa, however weird, found its share of believers. Africans were said to be unlike any people on earth. There were, for example, headless people with eyes, nose, and mouth in their chests. A tribe of pygmies, barely six inches tall, fought fierce battles with birds. Certain peoples had huge lower lips which they used as sunshades. Cannibals had heavy tails with which to knock their victims unconscious.

African wildlife was supposed to be just as strange. Sailors spoke in hushed tones of the roc, a gigantic bird able to carry off a full-grown elephant. There were sea horses that kicked boats to pieces and swallowed sailors whole. The rivers swarmed with "crocodiles that sob and weep like a Christian body,"[10] and when a Christian came to see what ailed them, they bit him in half. Finally, there was the oyster tree, from which hung millions of oysters instead of leaves.

The English saw no marvelous creatures when they arrived. Nor did they see many people, since the coastal tribes knew what whites wanted and ran off whenever they appeared. What they did see were piles of charred, cracked bones, evidence of cannibal feasts and human sacrifice.[11]

Three times the English tried to surprise sleeping villages, only to be surprised in return. They would land at night, sneak up on a village, and strike at dawn. But the village was empty. Moments later, hundreds of warriors burst from cover. The blacks were naked except for a strip of cloth wrapped around their waists. Pieces of bone were thrust through pierced ears and noses, and they wore necklaces of teeth from enemies they had killed. To make themselves look even more fearsome, their own teeth had been filed to sharp points.[12] Though armed only with wooden clubs and fire-hardened arrows, they drove off the invaders. On one occasion eight Englishmen died painfully after being slightly wounded by arrowheads dipped in a slow-acting poison.

Hawkins managed to collect 150 slaves, not enough to be worth a voyage to the New World. Things looked grim, until he was approached by three local chiefs. The chiefs were at war with Conga, a town of over eight thousand inhabitants on the Sierra Leone River. They had been at war on and off for several years, but Conga was so strong they had given up trying to take it until Hawkins appeared. In exchange for his help, they promised to give him all the slaves he wanted.

Two days later, the fleet anchored off Conga. The sailors stared in amazement. What they saw was no simple farming community. It was a fortress surrounded by a wall ten feet high. The wall was made of huge tree trunks bound together with vines and sharpened at the top. Platforms along the inside of the wall were crowded with men singing war songs and daring their enemies to attack. From the center of the town came the throbbing of drums and the chanting of women urging warriors to fight to the end.

The English led off by landing boatloads of sailors on the riverbank. Each man wore a steel helmet and a padded leather jacket. Some carried pikes, steel-pointed spears fifteen feet long. Others were armed with bow and arrow or an arquebus, an early type of musket.

As they came ashore, the ships' gunners swung into action. Tree trunks splintered under the impact of iron cannon balls, opening gaps in the wall. That was all the sailors needed. They burst into the town, setting fire to the huts as they advanced. With fires raging behind them, the defenders left their positions on the wall, allowing the three chiefs to break through on the landward side.

What followed was a living nightmare. While the English rounded up slaves, their allies went on a killing spree. They were not after prisoners, at least not just yet. They wanted blood, and blood is what they got. Anyone they met—man, woman, or child—was cut down on the spot. Townspeople panicked, not knowing where to go or what to do. Everywhere they turned they faced raging flames and bloodthirsty enemies.

The English were astonished at what happened next. Years later, a sailor named Job Hortop told of seeing crowds of people herded toward a swamp alongside the river. Once there, "the three kings drove seven thousand Negroes into the sea at low water, at the point of the land, where they were drowned in the ooze, for that they could not take their canoes to save themselves."[13] After that, things began to calm down. The victors rounded up their prisoners and made camp for the night. Hawkins had 250, the three chiefs another six hundred, of which Hawkins was entitled to a share.

The English were hungry after the day's fight, but they soon lost their appetites. They had camped outside the town and were cooking supper when some of their comrades appeared. The men were pale and shaken. They had been inside the ruined town, where the three chiefs were camped. The victors were holding their version of a thanksgiving dinner. Hundreds of prisoners had been butchered and their flesh roasted over open fires. The flesh was being eaten not because it tasted good, but as a way of magically capturing the enemy's strength. On the African plains, hunters ate the hearts of lions for exactly the same reason.

The chiefs broke camp before morning, without sharing the surviving prisoners. Hawkins was angry. The Negro race, he said, is one in which "is seldom or never found truth."[14] These were strange words coming from him. Apparently, it was all right for him to steal people to sell half a world away, but wrong for others to cheat him out of his "rightful" share. In any case, he had four hundred "pieces of merchandise" aboard when he left for the Spanish Main on February 2, 1568.

Two months of sailing separated the Old World from the New; two months alone on the Atlantic without meeting another vessel. This was the "middle passage," the most dreadful part of any slaving voyage. Sailors became short-tempered and, if they forgot themselves, drew knives and paid the penalty. Sometimes, for "entertainment," they baited hooks with meat and fished for sharks. They were not after the meat, which was not considered proper food. They hated the big fish and enjoyed torturing them in ingenious ways. A sailor explained: "Every day my company took more or less of them . . . to recreate themselves, and in revenge of the injuries received by them; for they live long and suffer much after they be taken, before they die. At the tail of one they tied a great log of wood . . . from another they plucked out his eyes and threw him into the sea. In catching two together they bound them tail to tail, and so set them a-swimming;

another, with his belly slit and his bowels hanging out, which his fellows would have every one a snatch at [that is, he was attacked by other sharks and torn to shreds]."[15]

The slaves had nothing to keep them amused. Compared to what they endured, a sailor's life was a summer picnic. Black men lay naked on the rough wooden decks, chained together hand to hand and foot to foot; women and children were kept unchained in separate compartments. Packed into darkened holds, eating only boiled beans, they fell victim to a host of diseases. The worst was dysentery, a deadly form of diarrhea. People lay in their own filth, causing the ship to stink worse than ever; it used to be said "you can smell a slaver five miles away." Blacks died aboard Hawkins's ships; of that we can be sure. But we can never know exactly how many, since no one thought it necessary to keep a record.

*U*pon reaching their destination, Hawkins put on his usual act. He would anchor off a settlement, roll out his guns, and demand to trade in peace. The Spaniards turned out in force, retreated after a fierce "battle" in which no one got a scratch, and then bought his slaves. Trading took time, and sometimes a town was held "captive" for weeks. While the inhabitants haggled over prices, the sailors amused themselves in their off-duty hours. Small groups would go into the countryside to see the sights and hunt. In one place, says Job Hortop, they cut "a monstrous venomous worm" in half with an axe, in another they shot a snarling "tyger." Stalking crocodile, however, was the most thrilling sport. For bait, they used a dog with a hook tied under its belly. After a few tries, they caught a twenty-three-footer, which they skinned and stowed aboard their ship as a souvenir. Little did they know that neither it, nor most of them, would ever reach England.[16]

By September, the slaves had been sold and Hawkins set a course for Plymouth. The voyage had been a success, and no doubt Cousin Francis was thinking about how to spend his share of the profits. He was entitled to more money than he had ever seen in his life. A few more voyages like this and he would be a rich man with a fleet of his own. But he had counted his fortune too soon.

The fleet ran into a hurricane off the western tip of Cuba. Though the other ships were slightly damaged, the *Jesus* was in terrible shape.

LA VERRA CRVS

Old to begin with, she leaked from every joint. A crewman described how the planks in her stern (rear) "did open and shut with every [wave] . . . and the leaks so big as the thickness of a man's arm, so that the living fish did swim upon the ballast as in the sea."[17] The only thing to do was to put into a harbor for repairs.

One gray September morning, a line of ships anchored off San Juan de Ulua, an island in the harbor of Vera Cruz, the chief port of New Spain. It was the busiest time of year in the port. Twelve treasure ships loaded with gold and silver lay offshore, waiting to join their escorts for the voyage across the Atlantic. Townspeople expected the escorts to arrive any day from Spain. Besides their regular cargo of trade goods, the ships would be bringing the incoming viceroy of New Spain, Don Martín Enríquez, a nobleman of enormous wealth and influence.

When the ships appeared, two officials came out to greet the viceroy in a small boat. Had he not been expected, perhaps the officials might have been more cautious. Spanish ships, particularly those carrying high officials, always displayed every bit of colored cloth in their lockers. But only one of the newcomers flew a flag, and it was so faded

VERA CRUZ, THE CHIEF PORT OF MEXICO, AS SEEN IN A SPANISH DRAWING OF THE SIXTEENTH CENTURY. THE ISLAND OF SAN JUAN DE ULUA LIES OFF THE MAINLAND, ITS SEAWALL RUNNING THE LENGTH OF THE HARBOR. THIS IS WHERE JOHN HAWKINS SUFFERED HIS WORST DEFEAT AND WHERE HIS YOUNG COUSIN, FRANCIS DRAKE, BECAME A LIFE-LONG ENEMY OF SPAIN.

that its markings could not be seen at a distance. Only when the officials came alongside and looked up did they see the lions and lilies of an English royal ship. Hawkins stood at the *Jesus's* rail, flanked by evil-looking fellows with drawn swords. Leaning over, a broad smile on his face, he invited the officials aboard as his "guests."

The ships raised anchor and made a beeline for San Juan de Ulua. Sixteen heavy guns lined the seawall, their crews standing at attention. As the English approached, they fired a salute while trumpeters sounded a greeting. Then they saw the lions and lilies. "The heretics are upon us," they shouted, fleeing their posts in panic. The rest was easy. English landing parties swarmed ashore to seize the island.

Hawkins was not looking for trouble. Once the island was secure, he wrote to reassure the *alcalde* of his peaceful intentions. He promised that no Englishman would set foot on the treasure ships; indeed, he would not hurt a hair on the head of any Spaniard. He merely wanted a few days to repair his ships and rest his men. He would pay handsomely, in gold, for any supplies he took.

Crews set to work, plugging leaks and mending torn sails. Repairs were going along well until, a few days later, a shout came from *Jesus's* crow's nest. "Sails ho!" the lookout cried, pointing out to sea. On the horizon, moving swiftly, were thirteen vessels advancing under full sail. The fleet consisted of eleven merchantmen escorted by two men-of-war, each with five hundred men, sailors and soldiers, plus dozens of heavy cannons. Don Martín Enríquez had arrived.

Hawkins had a problem. He would gladly have left before the Spaniards drew near, but *Jesus* was still in no condition to sail. Outnumbered and outgunned, if he allowed them to enter, he would be at their mercy—and he knew how Spaniards treated captured heretics. He could have kept them out of the harbor, since his men held the guns on the seawall and could blow them to bits. But it was hurricane season, and keeping them out would be the same as wrecking them in the next storm. Besides, England and Spain were at peace. Driving Spanish ships away from their own harbor, much less firing on them, would have been an act of war and therefore treason. Only Queen Elizabeth could declare war, and she was determined to remain at peace with Spain.

Hawkins decided to admit the Spaniards, but not without a pledge of good behavior. After some hard bargaining, it was agreed that the English could occupy the island and control the seawall guns until repairs were completed. No armed Spaniards were to go ashore. And to make sure everyone kept their word, each side handed over to the other twelve hostages. Don Martín Enríquez promised to honor the agreement to the letter, as a gentleman should.

As a gentleman should! That could be interpreted two ways. It could mean, as Hawkins believed, that a gentleman always kept a promise. But that was not how the viceroy saw it. He was a proud Spaniard and a devout Catholic. He knew all about *Achines de Plimua*—Hawkins of Plymouth—that Protestant rascal who broke his king's laws. To him, the English were outlaws who had forced their way in at gunpoint. A gentleman was no more bound to keep his word to them than an ordinary citizen to keep a bargain with a mugger. So the moment the agreement was signed, he ordered his captains to plan a surprise attack. Until they were ready, he would smile at those he meant to destroy.

John Hawkins was a hard man to fool. Though the Spaniards seemed to be acting properly, things just didn't feel right. Yes, they were polite—but too polite. Whenever a Spaniard met an Englishman, he always had a bow and a smile for his *amigo,* his "friend." But whenever an Englishman approached a group of Spaniards, they stopped talking until he passed, or huddled together to laugh among themselves. At night, there were unexplained movements between their ships and the sound of steel rattling against steel. One night *Jesus*'s crew heard sawing aboard a warship moored close to their own vessel. At dawn they saw new gunports cut in the warship's side.

Hawkins was not taking any chances. He doubled his lookouts and prepared for action. The Spaniards did not keep him waiting long.

On September 23, Hawkins sat down to an early lunch in his cabin aboard the *Jesus.* Among his guests were some of the Spanish hostages. Just as the meal was being served, an English officer grabbed the arm of the Spaniard sitting next to Hawkins. In the scuffle that followed, a dagger fell out of the fellow's sleeve. No one doubted who was to be on its receiving end.

After ordering the Spaniards' arrest, Hawkins ran up on deck. He arrived in time to see one of the viceroy's aides wave a white kerchief from the bow of a merchantman anchored nearby. Instantly, hundreds of Spanish soldiers jumped onto the island from their ships. At that very moment, Spanish sailors, who had been visiting with the Englishmen on the seawall, drew daggers from under their doublets. All but three Englishmen fell mortally wounded. The three saved themselves by diving off the seawall and swimming the short distance to the ships. Among them was Francis Drake.

Drake's cousin was furious. "God and Saint George!" he cried. "Upon those traitorous villains! I trust in God the day shall be ours!"

At those words, sailors grabbed axes and long oars called sweeps. While some cut the ropes holding the ships to the seawall, their comrades pushed against it with the sweeps. *Jesus* and *Minion* began to inch away. They drifted perhaps a hundred feet when the closest Spanish vessels, the warships, came into range. The English fired first. They fired fast, and often, and true.

Cannon balls smashed into one of the warships. Nobody lived to explain what happened, but apparently a lucky shot set off some kegs of gunpowder. There was a sharp *whoof* followed by a thunderous *crash*. The warship exploded in a blinding flash, sending timbers, guns, and men hurtling into the air. Moments later, the shattered hulk settled on the harbor bottom. But since the harbor was shallow, she did not sink completely. She lay there, her main deck above the water, sizzling and spouting clouds of smoke. Another volley swept across the decks of Don Martín's man-of-war, the Spanish flagship. Scores of sailors were cut down by wooden splinters that flew about like huge razor blades; splinters always killed more men than did direct hits by cannon balls. The survivors abandoned ship, leaving the viceroy alone amid the wreckage. After the battle, the English claimed to have killed 540 Spaniards, most of them aboard the two warships.

Drake and his comrades fought bravely, but Hawkins was the heart and soul of the English effort. He was everywhere, shouting orders, helping the wounded, and leading by example. It was as if he had a charmed life. Cannon balls passed within inches of his head, but he never flinched. Pausing for a moment, he called for a cup of beer. Lifting it for all to see, he called to the gunners to do their duty and act like men. No sooner did he put the empty cup down, when a cannon ball knocked it overboard. The gunners gasped; they had nearly lost their commander, the one person they trusted to bring them home in safety. Seeing their concern he shouted: "Fear nothing! God who has preserved me from this shot will also deliver us from those villains."

By then, however, the Spaniards had gained the upper hand. Having taken the guns on the seawall, they turned them against the English ships. The guns were so close and so well placed that they could hardly miss. Hawkins's three smallest vessels were sunk. *Jesus* was crippled, her mainmast so badly weakened that she could not take sail.

Hawkins ordered Drake to anchor *Judith* out of range and await further orders; his vessel was too small to be of any help in the fight. *Minion* came alongside *Jesus*. Using the larger ship as a shield, their crews tried to salvage whatever they could.

The Spaniards decided to use fireships. A fireship was simply a vessel loaded with anything that could burn. The object was to set it ablaze and send it drifting toward a group of enemy ships in a confined space, such as a harbor.

Toward evening, two fireships bore down on the English. They came slowly, burning furiously from stem to stern. For the first (and only) time, Hawkins's men panicked. Without waiting to see if the fireships would really hit them, they cut *Minion* loose and cast off as fast as they could. Many of their comrades, not to mention much of the treasure, were left behind. Hawkins himself barely managed to leap aboard *Minion* as she pulled away. The fireships drifted ashore, burning up harmlessly.

It was a long night for both sides. The Spaniards prepared to finish the job in the morning. The English worked just as hard to sail at first light. At dawn, *Minion* was alone; Drake had left without orders. He anchored in Plymouth harbor after a four-month voyage, on January 20, 1569. Hawkins later said he "forsook us in our great misery." Yet this seems out of character for Drake, whose whole life shows that he was no quitter. Perhaps he misunderstood Hawkins's order, or left because he felt he could do nothing to change the situation. Whatever the reason, Hawkins bore him no grudge and the incident was forgotten.

Minion sailed with the morning tide. Though safe for the moment, everyone knew she was a death ship. Overcrowded, she carried *Jesus*'s survivors in addition to her own crew. She had two hundred men aboard, twice her normal crew, with little food and nearly empty water barrels. Sailors existed on a daily ration of two ounces of bug-infested biscuit and a cup of water. "Hunger," a survivor recalled, "compelled us to eat . . . cats and dogs, mice, rats, parrots and monkeys [the ship's mascots]. In short, our hunger was so great that everything seemed sweet and savory."[18]

Hawkins dared not enter a port anywhere in the West Indies. The Spaniards had traded with him only because he was strong and had what they wanted; now he had nothing but starving men. Indeed, capturing him would have been a feather in the cap of any *alcalde*, a sure passport to promotion. There was only one hope: half the men must be put ashore for the others to have even a slight chance of reaching home. If not, all were doomed.

On October 18, Hawkins gathered his men on deck. After explaining the situation, he asked for volunteers to stay behind in Mexico, promising to return for them the following year. The choice was free, and no one was forced to go or stay except for a few with special skills needed to run the ship. It was a difficult choice, but they slowly made up their minds. When the roll was called, just about half volunteered to go ashore. After saying their good-byes, they marched inland while their comrades put to sea.

Little is known about the voyage, except that each day was worse than the one before. Arriving at Plymouth on January 25, five days after Drake, *Minion* literally had a skeleton crew: only fifteen men were still alive. These, plus the fifty-five who came back with Drake, were all that remained of the four hundred who had sailed fifteen months earlier.

Of those left behind, only two ever saw their homes again, and that after escaping from more than twenty years in captivity. Hunger forced those from the *Minion* to surrender within a few days. The moment they fell into Spanish hands, they regretted their decision. The soldiers who marched them to Mexico City drove them like beasts, shouting, "March on, you English dogs! March, heretics and enemies of God!" Those captured aboard the *Jesus* were hung "by their arms on high posts until the blood burst out of their finger ends."[19]

All were handed over to the Spanish Inquisition. This dreaded organization had been created in 1468 to investigate religious crimes and punish heretics. It operated in secrecy. Prisoners were kept in secret prisons, where questioning went on without letup. There was no idea of being innocent until proven guilty. Your arrest was itself proof of guilt, because, it was said, the Inquisition never bothered the innocent. Nor did you have the right to remain silent; indeed, refusing to answer was further proof of guilt. The aim of the questioning was to get you to incriminate yourself and others. If you were stubborn, insisting on your innocence, or if your answers were unsatisfactory, the Inquisitors "put the question," a polite term for torture. You might have fire applied to the soles of your feet. Or you might be racked; that is, tied naked to a device that tightened ropes around your body. Or a rag was stuffed down your throat and soaked with water until you answered "correctly."

Sooner or later, everyone broke. Morgan Tillett, seaman, admitted under torture that Francis Drake had converted him to Protestantism. Tillett's comrades confessed to thinking bad thoughts, holding untrue beliefs, and worshiping God in an "improper" manner.

Although the Inquisition operated in secrecy, its punishments were carried out in public. Sentence was passed at an *auto-da-fé* (act of the faith), a ceremony held in a town's main square. The Inquisition used a rising scale of punishments. These ranged from fines for minor offenses to whipping and imprisonment for serious crimes. Heresy, the worst offense, was punished by as nasty a death as can be imagined. The heretic was tied to a stake surrounded by brushwood and burned. If he repented his sins at the last moment, the Inquisition granted him

THE INQUISITION MADE SURE PEOPLE IN SPAIN AND THROUGHOUT THE SPANISH EMPIRE DID NOT BECOME HERETICS. SUCH PEOPLE WERE USUALLY FORCED TO CONFESS GUILT AND THEN BURNED ALIVE IN PUBLIC AS A WARNING TO OTHERS.

the "mercy" of being strangled before the flames reached him. If not, he was burned alive.

Three of Hawkins's men went to the stake. The others were dragged through the streets of Mexico City with ropes around their necks. As they went, guards gave them two to three hundred lashes with leather whips. They were then turned over to trustworthy Catholics to learn their religion and to be put to work. Not that these Catholics approved of the Inquisition's methods. Miles Phillips, a sailor who later escaped, reported: "For many Spaniards . . . do hate and abhor the Inquisition, though they stand in such fear of it that they do not let the left hand know what the right is doing."[20]

The majority were eventually freed, married, and became prosperous, but they were not allowed to leave New Spain. After the whipping, a few were sent to Spain to complete their punishment. There the former slave traders were themselves enslaved. The lucky ones spent from six to twelve years chained to the oar of a Spanish galley and were then imprisoned for life. The unlucky ones slaved in the galleys to the end of their days.

CHAPTER II

The Treasure House of the World

I am not going to stop until I have collected the
two million crowns that my cousin John Hawkins lost
for certain at San Juan de Ulua.
— FRANCIS DRAKE, 1578

on Martín Enríquez's "victory" at San Juan de Ulua was to have unexpected results for his country, none of them pleasant. Little did he know that his action would send shock waves throughout the Spanish Empire and that eventually full-scale war would explode between Spain and England. But that lay twenty years in the future. Meantime, Francis Drake would do his best to add fuel to the fire.

Not much is known of Drake's activities in the months after his return aboard the *Judith*. It was said that he served in one of Her Majesty's ships in Irish waters and that he smuggled arms to the French Protestants, France having just begun the first of sixteen civil wars between Protestants and Catholics. Perhaps he did both, but there is no record of either. What is certain is that he took a wife. On July 4, 1569, he married a Plymouth girl named Mary Newman. It is equally certain that they spent little time together. Europe was changing, the world was changing, and Drake wanted to be part of the action.

Drake watched events across the English Channel with deep interest. During his teenage years, Protestantism had spread to the Low Countries, then a Spanish possession.[1] In 1566, as he prepared to sail

with Hawkins, Protestant mobs attacked Catholics and wrecked their churches in several Dutch cities. King Philip II was outraged. "I neither expect nor wish to be a lord of heretics," he snapped.[2]

The Inquisition was put to work against heretics and troops were sent to keep order. People, both men and women, were executed in droves. But King Philip was mistaken if he thought the Dutch would back down. Instead, they became the first Europeans to issue a declaration of independence. In the war that followed, towns became fortresses, each requiring a long siege if it was to be captured. Rebel seamen, the savage "Sea Beggars," swarmed into the English Channel. Using small, swift boats, they seized hundreds of Spanish vessels each year. Important passengers were held for ransom; ordinary folks went overboard with their hands tied behind their backs.

Drake admired the Dutch. He saw their cause as God's, and therefore the cause of England. Spain was already too powerful, a menace to every other nation, he believed. Philip II would never be satisfied. Each success would only make him more reckless, more willing to use force. The moment he destroyed the Dutch, he would turn on the

French Protestants and, in time, on England itself. Philip's power, therefore, had to be checked at any cost.

There was something else, something personal. Drake had lost everything at San Juan de Ulua. All he had worked for was gone because of Spanish treachery. He took this loss personally. Because Spaniards had wronged him, he considered himself at war with the Spanish king and the Spanish nation; indeed, with everything Spanish. It was his own private war, and he would fight it all the days of his life. He came to see himself as a crusader, God's instrument to cripple Spain. And if he grew rich at the enemy's expense, well, that was a sure sign of the Lord's favor.

The key lay with the very thing that made Spain so dangerous: American treasure. This was the lifeblood of Spain's war machine, the glue that held its empire together. Stop it at its source, and Spanish power would vanish.

Treasure flowed to Spain in two streams. One came from Mexico by way of Vera Cruz. Although extremely valuable, it was small compared to the wealth of Central America and Peru. Here were riches unlike any seen by European eyes. From the mines of Central America came chests filled with pure gold. From the offshore waters came thousands of blue-gray pearls. From Peru came the most fabulous treasure of all: sacks of emeralds and tons of silver bars.

These treasures had to make a long journey before reaching their destination. Each year they were brought by ship to the Isthmus of Panama. An isthmus is a narrow strip of land, bordered on each side by water, connecting two larger bodies of land; the Isthmus of Panama has the Caribbean Sea on the east and the Pacific Ocean on the west. Treasure was landed at Panama City on the Pacific coast. From there, mule trains carried it along a secret jungle trail to Nombre de Dios, "Name of God," on the Caribbean to await the fleet that would take it to Spain. This town was commonly known as the "treasure house of the world." How Drake learned of the trail, and when, are unknown. Until then, there is no record of any Englishman entering the Caribbean for the purpose of plunder. Drake, however, intended to make history. He meant to rob the treasure house under its defenders' very noses.

In order to begin, he had to sell his idea to those who would be paying the bills. To this day, nobody knows the name of any of his backers. Whoever they were, there is a good chance that Hawkins's name led the list. After San Juan de Ulua, Cousin John stayed away from the New World for nearly thirty years; his career was at home, running his business and, later, remodeling the Royal Navy. He may well have put up some of the money and brought other businessmen into the scheme. In return for their investment, they would receive a share of the profits. If the venture failed, they might lose their money; Drake and his men stood to lose their lives.

Drake knew the venture was risky and had to be carefully planned. In 1569, he made a secret voyage to study Nombre de Dios and how it might be attacked. Using two small ships, he explored the surrounding waterways and drew maps of the coast; he even visited the town, disguised as a Spanish sailor, to familiarize himself with its layout and find where the treasure was stored. That in itself took courage, since he spoke little Spanish.

On his second voyage, in 1571, he found a harbor about a hundred miles down the coast. Named Port Pheasant after the brightly colored birds that lived in the area, it was hidden by thick jungle, making it a perfect base. He lay low, except to capture a couple of small supply ships, which were taken to Port Pheasant. Before returning to England,

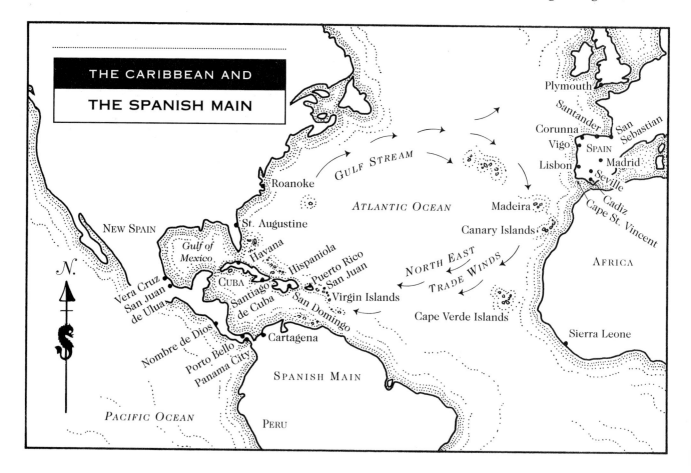

THE CARIBBEAN AND
THE SPANISH MAIN

he buried his extra supplies and freed the Spanish crewmen. Unlike other captains, Drake never harmed an enemy who could not harm him. He always freed prisoners, and even gave them gifts to make up for the trouble he had caused them.

On May 24, 1572, Drake sailed from Plymouth with the seventy-ton *Pasha* and the twenty-five-ton *Swan*. On board were seventy-three men, including his brothers John and Joseph. Except for the Drakes, no one knew their destination. Secrecy was essential, because the Spanish ambassador had spies in Plymouth, mostly Englishmen out for quick money. They hung around the waterfront, noting what ships were in port and eavesdropping on sailors' conversations. Any useful information was sent to their employer, who forwarded it to his master in Madrid.

Drake reached Port Pheasant on July 12. He had just taken his place in a longboat to be rowed ashore when he noticed a column of smoke rising from the forest. Immediately, he ordered an armed landing party to follow in another longboat. Upon landing, he found a huge tree on fire. Nailed to its trunk was a lead plate with an engraved message:

Captain Drake! If you fortune to come to this port, make haste away!
For the Spaniards which you had with you here the last year have
betrayed this place, and taken away all that you left here. I depart from
thence this present 7 of July, 1572.

Your very loving friend, John Garrett.[3]

Garrett was a Plymouth man who had been there and left five days earlier. With him were some of Drake's crew from the previous year. Having found that the Spaniards had visited the place, Garrett set the tree on fire as a warning signal.

But Drake was in no hurry to leave. It was not likely that he had been detected, and even if he had been, there was no immediate danger. He planned to stay at Port Pheasant only a few days. That was all he needed to prepare for the raid, strike, and disappear with the loot.

Once *Pasha* and *Swan* anchored in the harbor, the carpenters went to work. *Pasha* carried three "dainty pinnaces" shipped in parts that could easily be fitted together. A pinnace was a small, swift vessel powered by sails and sweeps, useful for scouting and running into shallow water to escape larger craft. Meantime, Drake worked alongside his men to clear land for a fort. It had no high walls, like Conga. Instead, trees were cut down and dragged into position at the water's edge. More trees were cut so that they fell on top of these, creating a barrier thirty feet high. There was a single narrow entrance, kept closed at night by a great tree drawn across.

Like a modern commando operation, Drake's plan depended upon surprise and split-second timing. They would approach Nombre de Dios just before dawn, while the inhabitants were still fast asleep. Once ashore, they would overpower the guards, storm the royal treasure house, and be gone before the Spaniards could react. If their timing was off, or something went wrong, they would be in deep trouble, since soldiers were stationed in the town. But if they succeeded, as Drake said they would, they would be rich. His words were music to the ears of poor men. A few hours of danger, they felt, was a small price to pay for a lifetime of comfort and prosperity.

The pinnaces set out on the afternoon of July 27. Hugging the coastline to avoid Spanish ships, they reached their destination after nightfall. Two miles outside the harbor, they dropped anchor and waited for dawn under a starless sky. They were young men—only one was over thirty. Most had never been in battle and hardly knew what to expect. As they sat waiting in their bobbing boats, their imaginations started to get the best of them. Nombre de Dios was no backward colonial village. "It is as big as Plymouth," they murmured, counting the house lights. Fear spread among them like a contagious disease.

Time seemed to stand still. Ten o'clock. Eleven o'clock. Midnight. One by one the lights went out and the town slept. All was quiet, except for the sound of surf washing against the shore.

Drake knew he must act before his men lost control. Suddenly the clouds parted and the moon peered out. Moonlight shone on the water, pointing to Nombre de Dios like a silvery finger.

That was all Drake needed. "The sun is rising. Daybreak is here. The time has come," he cried. The sailors, apparently, had not noticed that it was only three o'clock in the morning, a full hour before the planned assault. Without thinking, they began rowing toward the town. Rowing released tension, allowing them to master their fear.

Entering the harbor, they saw a ship riding at anchor, a wine carrier newly arrived from Spain. Just then a rowboat pulled away from its side. They had been seen and the ship's captain was trying to alert the town. The vessel must have been unarmed, since a cannon shot could easily have done the job.

Drake's luck held—at least for the moment. Quick as a flash, he went after the Spaniards. Gasping for air, their muscles straining, both crews rowed with all their might. The English were faster. As they drew near, the Spaniards got a good look at the strangers. It was enough to scare them out of their wits. There, in the moonlight, were bearded "savages" armed with swords and muskets. The Spaniards swerved aside and made for the opposite shore.

The English captured the seawall as soon as they landed. One after another the cannons mounted on it were knocked off their carriages; Drake was not taking any chances with seawall guns after San Juan de Ulua. Nevertheless, he had lost the element of surprise. The lone Spanish guard escaped, shouting as he ran toward the darkened town.

Raiders, though not the English, were expected and Nombre de Dios was not sleeping soundly. On and off, for many months, it had been attacked by bands of escaped slaves out to kill whites or kidnap them for torture in the jungle. The guard's shouts echoed through the empty streets. The blacks had returned!

His words struck like lightning bolts. Women screamed. Children wailed. A church bell set up a harsh clanging. Drum rolls came from the direction of the army barracks. Soldiers turned out in their battle gear. If Drake wanted treasure, he would have to fight for it.

Nombre de Dios was laid out like a typical Spanish town. In the center was a plaza where the main streets came together. Drake knew the defenders would rally there, and that he must drive them away in order

THIS DRAWING OF THE EARLY 1600S SHOWS NOMBRE DE DIOS (NAME OF GOD), THE TOWN IN PANAMA WHERE FRANCIS DRAKE TRIED TO CAPTURE A WHOLE YEAR'S TREASURE BEFORE IT WAS SHIPPED TO SPAIN.

to reach the treasure house beyond. He divided his men into two units. His brother John set out with seventeen men to sneak up on the plaza from the east. Drake led the larger group of about fifty men himself. He did not try to hide or move quietly; it was too late for that. His men came boldly down the main street, waving torches and shouting while a drummer and a trumpeter made as

much noise as they could. The idea was to trick the defenders into believing they faced a whole army.

Drake's men charged—straight into a volley of Spanish musket balls. The trumpeter fell dead at the captain's side. His comrades fell back, regrouped, and returned like a swarm of angry hornets. The result was a wild free-for-all in the dark. Men went at each other sword on sword, dagger on dagger. They were so close they could not reload after firing their muskets. Instead, they held them by the barrel and swung at each others' heads. It went on like this for about ten minutes. Finally, a burst of gunfire and a war cry came from behind the Spaniards. "Saint George for England!" shouted John Drake's men, coming on the run. The Spaniards panicked. Dropping their weapons, they fled down the side streets.

Drake grabbed a prisoner and, putting his sword to the fellow's chest, ordered him to lead the way to the governor's house. Its front door was open, a single candle flickering at the top of a long staircase. The English froze in their tracks, their eyes wide, their mouths open. There, shimmering before them, was a treasure unlike any their countrymen had seen since the beginning of the world. One Englishman recalled: "By means of this light we saw a huge heap of silver in that nether room; being a pile of bars of silver, as near as we could guess, seventy foot in length, of ten foot in breadth, and twelve foot in height, piled up against the wall. Each bar was between thirty-five and forty pounds in weight."[4]

Every one of those bars was worth more than a seaman earned in a lifetime. Eager hands reached out, only to be stopped by a sharp command. "No!" Drake cried. This was only silver; their true objective was the royal treasure house near the waterfront. This was stuffed with more gold and jewels than their pinnaces could carry.

As they hurried to the waterfront, a storm broke, forcing them to take shelter in a shed alongside the treasure house. The rain came down in sheets, driven by high winds. So near and yet so far! Not only were they soaked to the skin, their gunpowder was wet, leaving them almost defenseless. Off in the distance, they could hear Spanish war cries. The soldiers had rallied and were searching for the intruders.

Sailors began to mutter. They were outnumbered, said one, his voice quivering. Better return to the pinnaces before the trap closed, said another. Drake was furious at such cowardly talk. "I have brought you to the Treasure House of the World," he cried. "Blame nobody but yourselves if you go away empty."[5]

Hoping to inspire them with his own courage, Drake ran forward, only to fall flat on his face. He had been shot in the leg during the fight in the plaza, but he had refused to give in to the pain or tell anyone of the wound. Only now did his men realize that he had fainted from loss of blood. Looking down, they saw his bloody footprints in the sand and that his boot was filled with blood.

He revived quickly, but it was too late; the men refused to go forward. They were scared, but their fear was not only of Spanish steel and bullets. They were afraid of being stranded on the wrong side of the world. Drake was their captain. They trusted him, especially since only he knew how to navigate the Atlantic. Ignoring his commands, they bound his wound and carried him back to the pinnaces. Before leaving, they received more bad news. John Drake had broken into the treasure house, only to find it empty. A fleet had sailed with the gold and jewels just six weeks earlier. The whole effort had been for nothing.

The English retreated to an island outside the harbor to regroup before putting to sea. Next day, a messenger arrived from the governor of Nombre de Dios. A jolly little fellow, he praised their courage and offered to send them food as a token of respect for their courage. Drake knew he was a spy sent to discover their plans. They had whatever they needed, he said—everything, that is, except what they had come for. "I want only that special commodity [gold] which the country yields. Tell the Governor to keep his eyes open, for if God lends me life and leave, I mean to reap some of the harvest you get out of the ground and send to Spain to trouble all the earth."[6] The young man from Devon had only just begun to fight.

*D*espite Drake's defiance, the future looked bleak. There would be no second chance to surprise Nombre de Dios. No matter what his men thought, returning to England was out of the question for him. To return a failure would be the end of his career. No one would ever trust him with another ship. He would be a man without honor or respect, which for him was the same as being dead.

We do not know if he prayed, but what happened next was like the answer to a prayer. During the fighting in the plaza, a slave named Diego had escaped from his owner and fled to the pinnaces. Diego knew as much as any Spaniard about how their treasure was moved. Fighting was unnecessary, he said. It would be easy to capture a mule train in the jungle, *before* it reached Nombre de Dios.

Drake rejected the idea. His men were sailors, he said, not jungle fighters. No Englishman could survive in that tropical wilderness. They

THROUGHOUT THE
NEW WORLD, INDIAN
AND AFRICAN SLAVES
FLED TO FORM SET-
TLEMENTS IN THE
WILDERNESS. THESE
PEOPLE, KNOWN TO
SPANIARDS AS
CIMAROONS, OR "WILD
ONES," WAGED GUER-
RILLA WARFARE
AGAINST THEIR FOR-
MER OPPRESSORS.
THEY WERE ALSO
EAGER TO HELP ENE-
MIES OF SPAIN, SUCH
AS FRANCIS DRAKE.

would lose their way, wandering in circles until they starved or drowned in a swamp.

Diego knew better. He had friends who were as comfortable in the jungle as sailors were aboard ship. Known as the Cimaroon, they took their name from the Spanish for "wild" and "untamed."

The Spaniards found it difficult to keep slaves long enough for them to become profitable. "Of a thousand Negroes who arrive annually," the Bishop of Panama noted, "three hundred or more escape to the wilds."[7] There they intermarried with the natives, forming two new tribes. For half a century, these "black Indians" had fought a guerrilla war against their oppressors. No Spaniard was safe. Cimaroons might kill a traveler here, burn a farm there, and make nuisances of themselves everywhere. They were so bold they even slipped into settlements to coax away other slaves.[8]

Diego introduced Drake to the Cimaroon. Yes, they would be glad to help him against the Spaniards. Yes, they would lead him to the gold road. But what they could not understand was why he wanted the yellow metal. The Cimaroon valued iron for making weapons; gold was too soft to be useful for anything but ornaments. The only reason they captured it was to annoy the Spaniards, who worshiped it as a god. We can imagine Drake's feelings when they told of dumping whole mule-loads of it into swamps.

The bad news was that the rainy season had come, turning the jungle into a quagmire and closing the treasure trail. Nothing could be done until the rains ended in five months.

Drake used the time well. Port Pheasant was abandoned and a new base, Fort Diego, set up nearer to Cimaroon country. From there, he swept the sea for hundreds of miles to the north and south. Spanish coastal vessels were usually slow, clumsy, and unarmed. A pinnace would lie hidden behind a jungle-covered island. If a ship approached, the pinnace struck like a shark going after its prey. The Spanish ship was easily captured, looted, and sent on its way; no one on either side was killed or seriously wounded. Some ships were captured two or three times; indeed, it became almost a game for both sides. After a while, the Spaniards surrendered the moment a pinnace came alongside, knowing that no harm would come to them. Drake's tactics were so successful that he gathered supplies for a small army. He built four storehouses, thirty miles apart, so that if the enemy discovered one, there would still be plenty of food for his men.

Drake's boldest move was against Cartagena, capital of the Spanish Main. In the autumn of 1572, he played hide-and-seek with the Spanish authorities. Using two pinnaces, he would dart into Cartagena harbor, capture a ship as it was unloading its cargo, and take it out to sea to loot at his leisure. Try as they might, the Spaniards could not catch him. His pinnaces were too fast for that, and their crews had become seasoned veterans. Once, to show his contempt, he anchored close to a Spanish beach patrol. The patrol's leader invited him to come ashore and talk things over under a flag of truce. Drake landed alone, but would not come closer. "I have not enough strength to conquer you," he said, "but I have enough judgment to beware of you."[9] With that, he leaped into the rowboat and escaped.

Drake returned to find trouble at Fort Diego. Brother John had more courage than brains. He had attacked a Spanish ship filled with soldiers, his crew armed only with a broken-pointed sword, a rusty musket, and a fishing spear. John had the sword and a pillow as a shield when he led his men aboard the ship. He died in agony from a musket ball in his belly.

Soon after Drake's arrival, his men were struck by a disease, most likely yellow fever. Ten died, among them his brother Joseph. The survivors had no idea of the epidemic's cause. Some said it came from bad water, others blamed enemy witchcraft.

Although not a scientist, Drake realized that the only way to solve the problem was to look inside one of the victims. But when the men said this would be a sin, the human body being sacred, he offered his own brother. An eyewitness tells how Joseph "was ripped open by the surgeon, who found his liver swollen . . . and his guts all fair. This was the first and last experiment that our Captain made of anatomy in this voyage."[10] The surgeon, however, could not leave well enough alone. He invented a drug to prevent further infection and tested it on himself. It killed him.

At last the Cimaroon reported treasure ships at Nombre de Dios. The gold road was open once again.

Before setting out, Drake questioned Pedro, the Cimaroon chief, about the supplies he should take along. Pedro told him not to worry about food; his hunters would see that everyone ate well. Apart from their weapons, however, the English must have at least two extra pairs of shoes. Ahead lay a hundred miles through rugged terrain. They would be crossing swift rivers with sharp stones and gravel in their beds. Anyone without sturdy shoes would have his feet cut to ribbons. Drake ordered his men to repair their shoes and make spares out of leather brought from England.

On February 3, 1573, eighteen Englishmen and thirty Cimaroon stepped into the jungle. Each day they marched from sunrise until four o'clock in the afternoon, when they camped for the night. They marched single file, speaking only when necessary, and then in whispers. Pedro was not taking any chances; he knew from experience that in this country it was as easy to walk into an ambush as to set one. Four of his men went a mile ahead of the main party, breaking trail and leaving "road signs" for the rest to follow. These were easy to read if you knew the "alphabet" in which they were written. Every slash on a tree trunk, every set of crossed twigs on the path, had its own special meaning. For added safety, warriors marched alongside the English and a mile behind them.

For men of the Old World, the jungle was a wonderland. It pulsed with life. Clouds of blue-winged Morpho butterflies rose from the edges of mud puddles, where they gathered by the thousands to drink. Boa constrictors, fifteen feet long and a foot around, draped themselves on low branches, waiting to make a meal of any unsuspecting animal, even a small human. Higher still, brightly colored birds—red, green, yellow, orange, blue, violet—flew among the treetops.

The English marveled, and suffered. As long as they stayed under the jungle canopy, it was cool. But if they had to cross an open area, the sun hit them full force. Sweat rolled down their bodies, soaking their clothes as if they had been in a cloudburst.

As promised, food was no problem. There was plenty of fruit near the rivers—oranges, lemons, guavas—and potatoes for roasting. Cimaroon hunters brought in a steady supply of meat, generally wild pig. Once they served otter. When Drake turned up his nose at the dish, Pedro scolded him: "Are you a man of war, and in want, and yet doubt whether this be meat?"[11] Though he accepted the criticism, we do not know if he ate the otter.

Drake had befriended the black Indians as a means to an end. But the more he saw of them, the more he came to admire and respect them. They were good people. He never knew them to lie or steal. If an Englishman grew tired, they carried his pack. If one fainted in the heat, "two Cimaroons would carry him with ease between them," handing him over to others every two miles until he recovered. As they came to know him better, they told him about life under the Spaniards. They told of Cimaroon villages raided, of black people slaughtered or branded on the cheek and returned to slavery. That march through the Panama jungle was an education for Drake, as important as any of the lessons he learned at his father's knee. It was there that the former slave trader came to see blacks not as "merchandise," but as human beings. Never again would he traffic in human flesh.

The trail left the jungle and climbed into the mountains that form the backbone of the Isthmus. On February 11, they came to a high ridge midway between Nombre de Dios and Panama City. A giant tree with handgrips carved into its side stood alone on the crest. Pedro asked Drake to follow him, promising to show him something marvelous. Up they went, hand over hand. The wind blew hard in their faces, but they kept going until they reached a platform large enough for a dozen men.

To the east Drake saw the familiar blue of the Caribbean. But to the west was a sight never before seen by an Englishman. There, shimmering in the sunlight, was an expanse of green stretching to the horizon. It was Magellan's *Mar Pacífico*, the Pacific Ocean. Drake was so deeply moved that he fell to his knees, begging "Almighty God of His goodness to give him life and leave to sail once in an English ship on that sea."[12] Already he saw a vision of an adventure far more challenging than the capture of a mule train laden with gold.

After a while, he called his men to come up and see for themselves. They were impressed, as they would be by any curiosity, but they had no great desire to sail to the ends of the earth. Only John Oxenham, a Devon man who had become second-in-command, understood what Drake had in mind. Oxenham vowed that nothing would stop him from sailing the Pacific, "unless our Captain did beat him from his company."[13]

Three days later, they saw Panama City in the distance. Pedro dressed one of his men as a slave and sent him into town to gather information. He returned with good news. Three large mule trains would be leaving that very night. Two carried food and silver; the third, commanded by the treasurer of Peru, was laden with gold and jewels. It would be leading the way.

Sundown found forty-eight men hidden in the tall grass on either side of a jungle trail east of the city. Drake had ordered his men to wear white shirts so they would not attack each other in the dark.

It was one of those dreamy tropical nights, illuminated by a full moon and the Milky Way splashed across the sky. Fireflies flitted through the darkness, creating thousands of twinkling lights. The night was filled with the humming of insects and the croaking of tree frogs.

An hour passed. Two hours. The tinkling of bells came from the direction of the city. Closer. Closer. Closer. . . . it came by the minute.

Men tightened their grip on their weapons and peered from between blades of grass to catch a glimpse of their prey. Suddenly, the sound of hoof-beats came from the opposite direction. A Spaniard galloped down the narrow trail as if the devil was chasing him. Whatever had frightened the fellow, Drake thought, it couldn't have been his men; they were invisible in the grass.

The first mule train appeared. Drake blew a whistle and his men leaped from cover, shouting as they came. The Spanish guards dropped their weapons and ran away. It was that easy.

Eager hands dug into mule-packs, only to come out with vegetables. Drake was stunned. Only later did he learn that one of his sailors, named Robert Pike, had been drinking brandy to stiffen his courage. Instead, it made him stupid. As the rider came by, he stood up and waved his arms. A Cimaroon knocked him down and covered him with his own body, but it was too late. The Spaniard, seeing a "ghost" rising up in the moonlight, dug his spurs into his mount and sped down the trail—right into the arms of the treasurer of Peru. Suspecting an ambush by flesh-and-blood men, not ghosts, the treasurer put the food train ahead to trip the ambush while he returned to Panama City with the treasure.

"Thus, by the recklessness of one of our company," a raider recalled, "we were disappointed of a most rich booty, which is to be thought God would not [allow to] be taken, for that by all likeliness it was well-gotten by the Treasurer."[14] Drake agreed; the treasurer must have been an honest man for God to rescue him by means of a fool. There was nothing to do but return to base and start from scratch. It is not known what, if anything, happened to Robert Pike.

*D*rake was considering his next move when one of the pinnaces fell in with a French ship. Guillaume le Têtu, the ship's captain, was a Protestant raider and one of the finest mapmakers of the time. Têtu brought news of the St. Bartholemew's Day Massacre in his homeland. Six months earlier, on August 24, 1572, Catholics had killed thirty thousand Protestants in Paris—the only event known to have made the Spanish king laugh out loud.

The English were not amused. The massacre set their captain's blood boiling. Now, more than ever, he wanted revenge. He also needed help, since only thirty-one men were left of his original seventy-three. He and Têtu joined forces for another attack on the treasure road. This time, however, the plan was reversed. Rather than seize the mule trains at the start of their journey, they would strike when they neared their destination. It would be share and share alike, half the loot going to each side.

One night, the pinnaces landed thirty-five white men and their Cimaroon guides at the mouth of the San Francisco River near Nombre de Dios. While the strike force moved inland, the pinnaces left with orders to come back in four days; there was no point hanging around to attract attention.

Again there was a silent march through the jungle. Again the Cimaroon knew every step of the way. On the second night out, April 1, 1573, they camped a mile from Nombre de Dios. They were so close, and the night so still, that they could hear the carpenters working on the treasure ships in the harbor; repairs were always done in the cool of the night.

At dawn, they awoke to the familiar tinkling of mule bells. A Cimaroon scout had counted the mules and spoken to one of the black teamsters. Forty-five soldiers were guarding 190 mules, each with three hundred pounds of silver on its back; ten other mules were loaded with jewels and gold. This time there were no slip-ups. Drake's whistle sent his men into action with a whoop and a holler. The startled guards were only able to get off a few shots before running toward the town as fast as their legs could carry them. Some bullets, however, found their mark. One Cimaroon was killed and Têtu was hit in the belly.

The raiders collected their loot. Since there was too much silver to carry, they would have to return later; meantime, they hid at least fifteen tons in land-crab holes, under fallen trees, and along a riverbank. The black teamsters, all slaves, helped, "showing them where the gold was so that they should not play around with silver."[15] And it was lucky they did. Têtu was too badly wounded to escape, so two Frenchmen volunteered to stay with him until Drake returned. Spanish reinforcements soon captured Têtu and one of his men; the other escaped to tell the tale. They beheaded the captain immediately and forced his companion to show where the silver was hidden, then killed him as well. Most of the silver was dug up and carried to the king's treasure house in Nombre de Dios. The raiders, however, took all the gold, worth at least five million dollars in today's money.

After a two-day march, they reached the San Francisco River. But instead of finding three pinnaces, they saw *seven*, all Spanish. The Spaniards were heading toward Nombre de Dios from the very spot they were supposed to meet their own vessels, which were nowhere to be seen.

The pinnaces must have been sunk, said one sailor. Their crews had surely been tortured into revealing the location of their base, said another. A third begged God's mercy, for without it they were lost. Drake, however, refused to lose hope. He told them that even if God had allowed the Spaniards to sink their pinnaces, he had also littered the riverbank with the trunks of fallen trees. Those tree trunks could be made into a raft to reach their base before the enemy arrived. "It is no time to fear," he declared, "but rather to hasten to prevent what is feared."[16]

The men pulled themselves together. Working quickly, they built a raft with a sapling for a mast and a biscuit sack rigged as a sail. Drake then put to sea with one Englishman and two Frenchmen. As he pushed off, he waved good-bye and called: "I will, God willing, by one means or another get you all aboard [our ships] in spite of all the Spaniards in the Indies."

The sea was merciless. The four sat up to the waists in water, or up to the armpits at every surge of the waves. The combination of sun and salt water burned their skin, raising painful blisters. After six hours of torment, they saw the pinnaces, which disappeared into a cove without noticing them. Bad weather had prevented them from reaching the San Francisco in time.

The sun was setting when lookouts from the pinnaces saw four men running along the beach. Dressed in rags, they seemed frightened, often glancing over their shoulders as if an enemy was on their heels. Moments later, Drake came aboard one of the boats. Breathless, he had a look of terror in his eyes. Asked how things had gone, he frowned. He let the frown sink in for a moment, then flashed a smile. It had all been an act, a joke. Reaching into his shirt, he produced a bag of gold coins. Holding it out for them to see, he said, "Thank God, our voyage is made."

The rest was simple. Drake picked up the others and returned to base without incident. Since the pinnaces had outlived their usefulness, they were broken up and the ironwork given to the Cimaroon for arrowheads. After dividing the loot with the French and saying good-bye to his black friends, Drake and his men put to sea.

August 9, 1573, was a red-letter day in the history of Plymouth. It was a Sunday, and most of the townspeople were in St. Andrew's Church. The preacher had just begun his sermon when whispers rippled through the congregation: "Master Drake is anchored in the harbor!" Moments later, the church was empty as everyone ran to welcome him home. The young mariner was now a rich man. His sailors, those who survived, could live comfortably for years to come.

That could not be said for the Spaniards. Drake's raid had given them the shock of their lives. Yet it was only the beginning. He had not forgotten that day high in the tree facing the Pacific Ocean.

CHAPTER III

Around the World

*What English ships did heretofore ever anchor in the mighty
River Plate, pass the Strait of Magellan, range along
the coast of Chile, Peru and the backside of New Spain,
and traverse the mighty breadth of the South Sea?*
> —RICHARD HAKLUYT,
> *PRINCIPAL NAVIGATIONS, VOYAGES,
> AND DISCOVERIES OF THE ENGLISH NATION*, 1589

*D*rake had won the first round in his war with Spain. Only
it was still just *his* war. In spite of disagreements, England and Spain
were at peace, and in fact, Queen Elizabeth was making every effort
to patch up her differences with King Philip. Drake's success, therefore, was not merely a blow to peace, but an embarrassment to the
queen. Several of her chief advisers wanted him arrested and tried for
piracy.

That was a serious charge, for pirates, or corsairs, were not seen as
ordinary criminals. The law defined a pirate, in Latin, as *hostis humani
generis,* an "enemy of the human race." A pirate was so wicked that he
was unfit to live either on earth or water. He must be hung at high tide,
his feet dangling inches above the sea he had polluted. His body was
then to be cut down, chained to a post, and the tide allowed to rise and
fall over it three times. The remains were finally buried face down in
the mud below the high water mark, where the tides soon erased all
trace of his existence.

Unwilling to lose their profits, Drake's backers told him to disappear
until things calmed down. He did, and so completely that historians

can account for his whereabouts for only five months in the next four years. All we know is that he commanded a patrol boat off the Irish coast from May to October, 1575. Ireland was only a few hours sailing time from England, but for an Englishman it might as well have been on the other side of the world. England had conquered the island in the twelfth century, but the Irish, refusing to knuckle under to foreign rule, rebelled constantly. These uprisings had grown worse since the English had become Protestants while the Irish remained Catholic. In the latest "troubles," the rebels were aided by Catholics from Scotland, then an independent country. Drake's job was to guard the coast, preventing smugglers from bringing in supplies.

The details of Drake's activities remain a mystery, but whatever he did, it pleased his commander, Robert Devereux, earl of Essex. At the end of his tour of duty, Essex gave him a letter of introduction to Francis Walsingham, England's secretary of state. Mr. Secretary Walsingham was one of the most important men in England. Not only did he advise the queen on foreign affairs, but he was a master spy, the father of the British secret service. His "ears"—his agents—were everywhere, and it was said that he could hear in London what was whispered in Madrid. A staunch Protestant, he believed war with Spain was inevitable.

At their first meeting, Walsingham explained why he had called Drake to London. Relations with Spain had not improved; indeed, they were growing worse. King Philip would not listen to Her Majesty's pleas for peace in the Low Countries. Each day his armies advanced further, bringing with them all the horrors of the Inquisition. English seamen were also being seized in Spanish ports and thrown into Inquisition prisons. Even the queen herself was in danger. To her Catholic enemies, she was the "Jezebel of the North." Church leaders in Rome called for her assassination, claiming "there is no doubt that whosoever sends her out of this world with a pious intention of doing God service, not only does not sin but gains merit." Their call was supported by Spanish writers and quietly approved by their government.

Walsingham told Drake that he was the sort of man England needed at this critical time. Her Majesty wanted to send King Philip a message. It must be strong enough to warn him to mend his ways, but not so strong as to trigger a war. She hated war and would do anything to avoid it—anything, that is, within reason.

Spreading a map on the table, Walsingham asked Drake to mark the places where Spain might be hurt and to draw up a plan of action. The seaman refused to put anything down on paper. Queen Elizabeth was only human, he said. All people die when their time comes, but he had no intention of hurrying things along. If the queen should die and be succeeded by a ruler friendly to Spain, he would have signed his own death warrant. Nevertheless, he noted that the best way to annoy King Philip was "by his Indies," that is, in the New World. He would say nothing more. A few nights later, he received an invitation to join Walsingham at the royal palace. Drake was to meet Her Majesty in person.

As Walsingham showed him in, Drake saw a woman of forty-four with small black eyes, a slightly hooked nose, and a long chin. Her face was pitted with smallpox scars, and she wore a red wig, since the smallpox had also left her nearly bald. Her teeth were black, a common thing with the English, who ate excessive amounts of sugar. Though there is no record of what she wore on that occasion, it is well known that she enjoyed fine jewelry, and lots of it. Pearl earrings, diamond rings, gold bracelets, and ruby necklaces were part of her everyday outfit. She also loved brightly colored clothes and, as was the custom among unmarried English ladies, kept her bosom uncovered in public. A French visitor wrote in amazement: "She was strangely attired in a dress of silver cloth, white and crimson, or silver 'gauze,' as they call it. The dress had slashed sleeves lined with red taffeta, and was girt about with other little sleeves [tassels?] that hung down to the ground, which she was forever twisting and untwisting. She kept the front of her dress open, and one could see the whole of her bosom . . . Often she would open the front of this robe, as if she was too hot. . . . Her bosom is somewhat wrinkled . . . but lower down her flesh is exceedingly white and delicate, as far as one could see."[1]

Her Majesty may well have been the most educated woman in England. As a child, some of the nation's finest scholars served as her tutors. They had an equally fine pupil, for she easily mastered any subject. Elizabeth Tudor—to use her family name—wrote poetry, composed music, played the lute, and was fluent in seven languages: English, French, Italian, Dutch, Spanish, Greek, and Latin. After the St. Bartholomew's Day Massacre, she scolded the French ambassador for an hour in perfect Latin, without missing a word or pausing for breath.

Known as the "Virgin Queen," because she never married, Queen Elizabeth I ruled from 1558 to 1603. During her reign, England began to build an overseas empire and became the world's greatest naval power.

Her wisdom was legendary, admired by friend and foe alike. Pope Sixtus V paid her the highest compliment he could: "She certainly is a great queen and were she only a Catholic she would be our dearly beloved. Just look at how well she governs! She is only a woman . . . and yet she makes herself feared by Spain, by France, by the [German] Empire, by all."[2]

That included her own subjects. People said that when Queen Elizabeth smiled, it felt like sunshine in January. Nevertheless, storm clouds could blow in without the slightest warning. Her Majesty's temper tantrums were feared throughout the realm. She would stamp her feet, curse, and threaten to make those who had displeased her "shorter by a head." She slapped advisers' faces and threw shoes at their heads; even Walsingham was hit once or twice. Her words stung like wasp stings. When, for example, a nobleman accepted a medal from the king of France, she made him give it back. "My dogs wear my collars," she sneered.[3]

The queen knew how to handle men of action. They must not be bullied but, rather, made to feel needed. "Drake," she said, coming to the point at once, "I would gladly be avenged on the King of Spain for divers injuries that I have received."[4] It was music to his ears. Then and there, they worked out a plan of action. The details of it were written down, but the document was badly burned in a library fire a hundred years later. Yet from the remains, and from Drake's own actions, we can get a good idea of its contents.

Drake knew the Spaniards felt secure on the western coast of South America. Since no foreign vessel had ever been there, their settlements were poorly defended and their ships lightly armed. The plan probably did not call for him to sail across the Pacific, much less circumnavigate the globe. No one in their right mind would have made such a voyage

plowing ahead when schools of them suddenly rose out of the sea, trying to escape the dolphins that fed on them. Many landed on the ships' decks, and the sailors used them as bait to catch the dolphins. Fresh dolphin was a pleasant change from salt beef and codfish.

On April 5, 1578, they came to a part of the Brazilian coast called *Terra Demonum,* "Land of Demons." This area has always been a grave-yard of ships. According to legend, long ago the Portuguese tried to enslave the local people, but they failed, because the Indians made a pact with the devil. In exchange for their souls, the devil taught them

AROUND THE WORLD WITH FRANCIS DRAKE! IN THIS CHARMING WOODCUT PORPOISES FORCE FLYING FISH TO TAKE WING AND LAND ON THE DECK OF DRAKE'S SHIP.

everything he knew about magic. They learned how to brew fogs, send hurricanes, and move sandbanks "both for a revenge against their oppressors and also for a defense."[8] Having never seen other Europeans, they believed all ocean-going ships belonged to the hated Portuguese. That, the English thought, explained why they nearly ran aground in a fog. It had been a close shave, with one vessel actually scraping its bottom on submerged rocks.

The grumbling continued as the squadron anchored in the River Plate near present-day Buenos Aires, Argentina. After refilling his water barrels, Drake coasted southward for several hundred miles to Port Saint Julian. This desolate place was as famous as its reputation was evil. There Magellan had executed mutineers during his own voyage; the only trace of his visit was the gallows on which they were hung. Everyone knew the story.

Ordering the ships to keep a safe distance, Drake went ahead with a landing party. As they came ashore, a group of Indians appeared from behind the rocks. Young warriors, they carried bows and arrows. Drake held out some presents, which they accepted, smiling and pointing to one of his men. The fellow carried an English longbow, a powerful weapon twice the size of their own. Using sign language, they challenged him to a shooting contest. He drew the bow and *whoosh*, an arrow flew down the beach. An Indian shot next, but his arrow went barely half as far. Just then other warriors appeared. Older men, they were shouting and waving their arms; the leader was beating a small dog he carried so that it would bite the strangers. Clearly, they were not welcome.

Drake told his men to lower their weapons, not wanting to provoke a fight. It was too late. The archer, not realizing the danger, meant to take another shot. He had already fitted a fresh arrow to his bow and was drawing the string back to his ear when it broke. Instantly, the newcomers let loose a hail of arrows. Blood gushed from the archer's mouth and nose as he fell mortally wounded, shot through the lungs. A sailor named Oliver stepped forward with a musket, the landing party's only firearm. He was taking aim when an arrow pierced his heart.

Drake sprang into action. He ran to Oliver's body, grabbed the gun, and fired a load of buckshot into the Indian leader. The man appeared to explode as the pellets hit him. They "tore out his belly and guts, with great torment, as it seemed by his cry, which was so hideous and horrible a roar."[9] His companions had never seen a musket, much less what it could do at close range. Now they knew. They ran away and never came back.

Drake turned to more pressing business. Thomas Doughty had not realized the kind of man he was up against. Once Drake set his mind to anything, he was ruthless. He might forgive stupidity, but anyone who deliberately stood in his way was doomed. On July 16, he selected a forty-man jury to hear the case against Doughty. The charge: mutiny. The penalty: death. No one doubted what the verdict would be.

Doughty rightly claimed that he had never planned a mutiny, and therefore had broken no law. Drake, however, cared nothing for what he called "pretty" legal arguments. He replied that deeds alone do not make a traitor; words and attitudes can have the same practical effect. The accused must not only answer for treachery against his commander, but against Queen Elizabeth whose servant he was. And that was treason.

Drake appealed to the jury's self-interest and patriotism. The trial was really about the future, not the past. "Just think, what would become of you if I were dead?" he asked, looking each man in the eye. "You would fall to fighting among yourselves. And do not imagine that you would ever find your way home without me to lead you. Think carefully about this voyage we are embarked upon. So great an enterprise has never been sent forth from England. If it succeeds the humblest sailor here will return home a gentleman. But if we do not proceed with this voyage, if we turn tail for home, think of what a laughing stock we shall be and what dishonor we shall bring upon our country. But I tell you, I do not see how this voyage can continue if this fellow is allowed to live. Well, my masters, what do you think? If you say that Thomas Doughty is worthy to die, hold up your hands?"[10]

Forty hands rose as one.

Drake allowed Doughty to choose the method of execution: hanging, shooting, or beheading. This was viewed as a courtesy owed to any gentleman. In the sixteenth century, it was considered a privilege to die the "right" way. Hanging was "for dogs and not for men," that is, not for gentlemen. The rope was painful, the victim dying by slow strangulation rather than having his neck broken. A bullet was quick, a real blessing. Beheading, however, was the method of choice. True, it was messy, but that was not the victim's concern; it was also painless if done correctly. For centuries, the axe had been reserved for the well-born, including royalty; King Henry VIII had sent two of his six wives to the headsman.

The day after the trial, Drake and his officers gave Doughty a farewell banquet. Each guest played his role as expected. They ate a hearty meal, drank to each other's health, and made little jokes; it was bad manners to mention what was coming. The meal over, Doughty and Drake prayed together and embraced as friends. Then an officer led Doughty to the chopping block. He went willingly, head high and hands untied, as a gentleman should.

"Strike clean and with care, for I have a short neck," Doughty told the executioner, who wore a black mask. As was customary, the doomed man gave the executioner money as a token of forgiveness and to insure a neat job. Then, kneeling, he put his head on the block. A second later, his headless body lay twitching on the ground.

Drake picked up the bloody head by the hair and held it high.

"Lo, this is the end of traitors," he cried.

A month was spent in preparing for the next stage of the voyage. There was plenty to do. *Swan* and *Benedict* were unloaded and sunk; they were very small and had served their purpose as carriers of extra supplies. The remaining ships, however, were in no condition to go further. That was normal after months in tropical waters. They had been at sea long enough for their bottoms to have become fouled with seaweed and infested by naval worms, creatures that bored deep holes in the wooden planks.

In order to repair a ship, it had to be careened. At high tide it was run aground sideways to the beach. Wooden ramps were then built in the sand close to its side and ropes attached to the tops of the masts. At a signal, everyone hauled and drew (pulled) on the ropes, tipping the vessel on its side and exposing its bottom. Work crews scraped the bottom clean, replaced rotten timbers, filled worm holes, and caulked seams wherever necessary. When they finished, the process was repeated on the opposite side. The swabber and liar went through the ship squashing bugs, killing rats, and generally cleaning up. Careening was hard, dirty work, and no one liked it, least of all the gentlemen. They refused to help.

That was the last straw. One Sunday, the company gathered to hear Chaplain Fletcher preach a sermon. But as he stood up, Drake waved him aside; he would deliver the day's sermon. He began by telling them that, while not learned in books, he spoke plain English and wanted everyone to listen carefully. There had been too many bad words between gentlemen and sailors. He was sick of it and wanted it to stop. "My masters," he said, his voice rising, "I must have the gentleman to haul and draw with the mariner, and the mariner with the gentleman. I would know him who would refuse to set his hand to a rope."[11] He then offered to give a ship to those who wished to turn back, promising to sink them if they ever crossed his path. No one took the offer, because they had come to accept his authority without question.

Drake's sermon was a triumph both for him personally and for a larger principle. It was not a call for democracy or equality. These have nothing to do with running a ship on the high seas. It was, rather, a demand for professional recognition, a very modern idea. What he meant was that a ship, especially a warship, could only have one commander, and he must be a mariner. The handling of a ship, no matter how difficult or dirty, is a skilled occupation regardless of its members' social standing. Ability, not birth, is what counts at sea. Sailors, though lowborn, deserved respect not for who their parents were, but for themselves and what they did. Drake's rule was first accepted by the English, then the Dutch. The result would be seen when the Spanish Armada, crowded with noblemen, sailed up the English Channel ten years later.

*T*hey reached the Strait of Magellan on August 21, 1578. Before entering, Drake marked the occasion by renaming his flagship the *Golden Hind* in honor of one of his backers who had a golden deer on his coat of arms. After praying to God for success, he set sail for the west and the wide waters beyond.

What a sight! Towering mountains rose on either side of the strait, their slopes covered with glaciers and snow fields, their peaks soaring upward, vanishing into the clouds. Icy winds swept down the mountainsides, kicking up funnels of dry snow and sending waves crashing into the ships.

On the third day, they came to three islands, the largest of which Drake named Elizabeth in honor of the queen. This island had colonies of flightless birds that the Welsh sailors called "whiteheads," or *pen gwyns*. "Their color [is] somewhat black, mixed with white spots under their belly and about their neck," Chaplain Fletcher observed. "They walk so upright that afar off a man would mistake them to be little children. If a man approach anything near them they run into holes in the ground."[12] Sailors pulled them out with hooks tied to the ends of sticks, then clubbed them over the head. Three thousand were killed, enough to last seven weeks. They found the penguin meat tasty, and none of the birds weighed under ten pounds. On another island, two hundred seals were killed in an hour. Having seen few humans, they had no reason to fear them. Sailors walked right up to them with their clubs and axes.

Elizabeth Island was inhabited by nomads, people who settled in one spot until they used up the natural food and then moved on to the next. These were hardy folks. The English were bundled up against the piercing cold and dampness, and still their teeth chattered. In contrast, the nomads went stark naked, their only covering being paint made from seal fat and the juice of berries. Some painted their bodies completely black; others added white stripes, yellow suns, and red circles. Chaplain Fletcher believed the paint kept them warm, since it "doth fill up the pores so close that no air or cold can enter."[13] Everyone marveled at the nomads' tools. Knives were the shells of giant mussels, each a foot long, the edges rubbed razor-sharp on stones. Buckets, cups, and boxes were made of tree bark sewn with seal gut. Their bark rowboats were so graceful and well made that the strangers thought them more fit for princes than poor wanderers.

On September 6, they left the Strait of Magellan behind. That in itself was a major accomplishment. In 1520, Magellan had taken thirty-seven days to pass through the channel. Drake did it in just sixteen, a record that stood for over a century.

El Mar Pacífico, "Peaceful Ocean," is what Magellan had called it; in Latin it was *Mare Pacificum*. When he first saw it years earlier, it really was peaceful. This time, however, the Pacific showed the English a very different face. To them, it was *mare furiosum*, "furious ocean," and "ocean of sorrows." No sooner did they arrive, than a storm roared in from the west. Sailors are used to storms; they come with the job. Yet no one had ever imagined anything like this monster. For fifty-two days, from September 7 to October 28, it was like the biblical Flood, only they were not sure that God was with them as He had been with Noah. "God," Chaplain Fletcher wrote, "seemed to set Himself against us . . . as if He had pronounced a sentence not to stay His hand . . . till he had buried our bodies, and ships also, in the bottomless depth of the raging sea."[14]

The sea sounded like thunder, rolling and churning and tossing them "like a ball in a racquet."[15] The wind shrieked in the rigging, tearing sails to shreds. Masts shuddered and bent, as if about to snap in two. Ships climbed sixty-foot waves, then spumed down the other side on a mad roller coaster ride. Decks were awash, making it necessary to rig lifelines; anyone who could not grab a rope when a wave struck was sure to be swept overboard. And there could be no stopping for rescue. Below decks, the guns were tied securely; a gun breaking loose and rolling around could smash anything in its path, even break through a ship's side. We still call a reckless person a "loose cannon."

Sailors lost track of time, minutes seemed like hours, hours like days. There was no day or night, only darkness and rain. It was always the same: work until your muscles ached and your head buzzed from fatigue. The men worked by candlelight, up to their knees in water, securing bundles, and bales, and barrels. They worked the pumps for ten-hour shifts, then lay down on the wet boards to sleep in their wet clothes. Sometimes they were given beer and biscuit, but no hot food, since the galley fire was put out when the storm began.

After three weeks of struggle, *Marigold* went down with all hands, twenty-nine men. Their screams could be heard above the roar of the storm. A week later, *Golden Hind* and *Elizabeth* became separated at night. Thinking Drake lost, *Elizabeth*'s captain sailed back through the strait for home. That in itself was a magnificent piece of seamanship, since the eastward passage is still regarded as the most dangerous.

Golden Hind was driven six hundred miles to the south. Finally, she anchored in the lee of an island, the side sheltered from the wind. She was there when the storm ended on the fifty-third day.

But this place was not supposed to exist. Geographers at that time thought the Strait of Magellan lay between South America and a vast, yet-to-be-discovered continent that completely circled the globe; they were so sure it existed that they put it on their maps. Drake had such a map in his sea chest.

Looking to the south, however, he saw no land whatsoever. Suddenly he realized that all the geographers and all their maps were wrong. There was only open water, where the Atlantic and Pacific joined to form a single super-ocean. He had discovered a new route around South America south of the Strait of Magellan. Three centuries later, before the opening of the Panama Canal in 1914, Yankee merchants and gold-seekers would take that route to the riches of

California and the Far East. Drake went ashore. He lay flat on top of a cliff and reached out as far as he could, putting himself further south than anyone in recorded history.

DRAKE LANDS ON MOCHA ISLAND ON THE FIRST LEG OF HIS VOYAGE AROUND THE WORLD. NOTICE THAT THE INDIAN ON THE RIGHT HAS TAKEN THE COMMANDER'S HAT AND IS RUNNING AWAY WITH IT.

*G*olden Hind turned northward. On November 25, she reached Mocha Island off the coast of Chile. Mocha was inhabited by Indians who had fled the mainland to escape Spanish slavery and torture. Spaniards who fell into their hands were exterminated like vermin.

Drake was warmly received by the Mochans. In exchange for some cloth and colored beads, they gave him chickens, vegetables, and two

fat sheep. Although he warned his men to speak only English or use sign language, several said they needed *agua,* Spanish for water. The Indians looked at them strangely for a moment, then promised to lead them to a fine spring when they returned.

Next morning, twelve men and their captain rowed to the island. On the beach was an Indian "welcoming" committee. Sailors Tom Brewer and Tom Flood ran ashore with a rope to secure the boat. Suddenly, some of the welcomers seized the sailors, while others grabbed the rope and began pulling the boat higher onto the beach. At that moment, scores of Indians came from behind rocks with bows and arrows.

Huddled together in their tiny boat, the English were perfect targets. Every man was hit several times; one fellow was a pincushion with twenty-five arrows sticking out of his back and chest. Drake was hit twice; one arrow grazed his scalp, another struck his face under the right eye near the nose. They would have been slaughtered had not a quick-thinking sailor cut the rope with an axe, allowing a wave to carry the boat back to sea. By some miracle, only one man died of his wounds aboard the *Golden Hind*; the others soon recovered. Fortunately, the Indian arrows were made of thin reeds tipped with stone points. Unlike English arrows, made of solid wood tipped with iron, they lacked penetrating power.

Drake sent another boat to rescue Brewer and Flood. It was impossible. As the boat neared shore, hundreds of Indians lined the beach, howling and waving weapons. They were having a "feast," and did not wish to be disturbed.

The English could scarcely believe their eyes. Their screaming comrades lay on the ground, feet and hands tied, while the revelers danced around them. Slowly, carefully, other Indians were tearing them to pieces. "Our men were in their execution and torments," an eyewitness recalled. "The tormentors, working with knives upon their bodies, cut the flesh away in gubbets, and cast it up in the air. The which, falling down, the people catched in their dancing, and like dogs devoured in most monstrous and unnatural manner . . . and thus continued till they had picked their bones, life yet remaining in them."[16]

Returning to the ship, the boat's crew demanded revenge. The Mochans were eating English flesh; very well, let them also taste English iron. *Golden Hind*'s big guns must go into action at once.

Drake refused. The Indians, he said, were not entirely to blame for the tragedy. By using the word *agua,* his men had led them to believe they were Spaniards, and they were now receiving "a Spaniard's reward."[17] The deed was done; killing Indians would not bring their comrades back. The only thing to do was to weigh anchor and find the common enemy.

The search proved easier than expected. Though battered and alone, the English were in the Pacific with a powerful warship. Drake's arrival took the Spaniards by surprise, and news traveled slowly. Heading north along the cost of Chile and Peru, Drake struck again and again. His first target was Valparaiso, Chile. On December 5, he entered the harbor under full sail. The *Grand Captain of the South Sea*, a Spanish vessel bound for Panama with four chests of gold and a large cross decorated with emeralds, was riding at anchor. She was not expecting company, but when *Golden Hind* appeared, her crew opened wine bottles and prepared for a fiesta. It was not to be. The moment the stranger came alongside, armed sailors clambered over the rails shouting "*Abajo perros!*"—"Down, you dogs!" The astonished crew was hustled below and the hatches closed over them. The boarders then took the valuables and, for good measure, loaded up on food and wine.

From then on, it was smooth-sailing all the way. Drake, it seemed, could put a raiding party anywhere on the coast and have it return with treasure. At one place, for example, they found a Spaniard asleep under a tree with thirteen bars of silver at his side; they took the silver without waking him. Elsewhere, they met a Spaniard driving eight mules, each loaded with a hundred pounds of silver. No, that could not be, said the Englishmen with mock sympathy. "We could not endure to see a gentleman Spaniard turned carrier," they explained later, "so we offered our services and became drovers, and almost as soon as he had parted from us we were come to our boats."[18]

At Callao, the port of Lima, capital of Peru, Drake put on a dazzling show. On the morning of February 15, 1579, *Golden Hind* swept into the crowded harbor and dropped anchor. Before the eyes of astonished onlookers, he jumped into a longboat to "pay his respects" to the Spanish ships. Visiting each in turn, he took what he wanted and cut the anchor cables, letting them drift out to sea with the tide. Satisfied at last, he calmly sailed away.

Drake, too, had a surprise at Callao. He learned that a magnificent treasure ship had left for Panama two weeks earlier. Her name was *Nuestra Señora de la Concepción,* "Our Lady of the Conception," after the Immaculate Conception of the Virgin Mary. Her crew called her

Cacafuego, "Spitfire," because she carried many small cannons. Heavy guns were scarce on the Pacific coast of South America; besides, her captain, San Juan de Antón, did not expect an attack from anything larger than native canoes.

Drake clapped on every rag of sail his masts could hold and sped northward. Up in the crow's nests lookouts scanned the sea, eager for the gold chain he promised to the first man who saw the prize. Now and then, he captured coastal vessels to renew his supplies and get information on *Cacafuego*'s progress. The crews were always released without harm.

On March 3, the captain's teenage nephew, John, claimed the reward. Up ahead, moving slowly, he spotted *Cacafuego* off Cape San Francisco, Ecuador. She had just crossed the equator and her captain was taking it easy. No need to hurry; he felt safe in the Pacific, which was merely a Spanish lake.

Drake could have caught up easily, but that would have meant a fight, something he'd rather avoid. He planned to strike at sundown, when he could move in close without the Spaniards noticing that *Golden Hind* was a warship. To do this, he had to gain on *Cacafuego* gradually. He ordered full sail, but also had a line of wine barrels filled with water strung out behind the stern. These acted as a drag, making *Golden Hind* seem like an overloaded merchantman struggling to make headway.

San Juan de Antón watched the stranger inch up on him throughout the day. Antón thought that perhaps she brought a message from Peru. Curiosity finally won out and, toward sundown, he turned around and sailed into Drake's trap.

As the distance between them closed, Drake cut the wine barrels loose. *Golden Hind* shot forward, drawing alongside *Cacafuego* in a matter of minutes.

Her captain was leaning over the rail to take a better look when he heard a shout. "Strike sail, Mr. Juan de Antón; if not, look out, for you will be sent to the bottom." Drake was demanding that he lower his sails as a sign of surrender.

"What England is this [to give me orders] for striking sail?" replied the proud Spaniard. "Come on board to strike sails yourselves!"

The answer was the shrill sound of a whistle, the same one that had sounded near the gold road, and the roll of a drum. Then hell broke loose.

Caca Fogo.   Caca Plata.

Musket balls swept across the Spaniard's deck. Arrows whipped overhead. Guns sent chain-shot, two iron balls joined by a chain, twirling through the air. *Cacafuego*'s mizzenmast—the rear mast of a three-masted vessel—fell in a tangle of rope and canvas. Englishmen leaped onto the ship, each with a sword in one hand and a pistol in the other. The crew, stunned by the fury of the attack, ran below, leaving their captain to face the boarders alone. The English were unhurt; a few Spaniards were wounded, but none killed.

San Juan de Antón was taken aboard the *Golden Hind*. There he saw Drake wearing a steel helmet and breastplate. He looked more fearsome than he really was. The moment Drake saw his prisoner, he embraced him, saying: "Have patience, for such is the usage of war." Note the word "war": though

AFTER AN ALL-DAY CHASE, DRAKE IN THE GOLDEN HIND CAUGHT UP WITH THE CACAFUEGO OFF THE WESTERN COAST OF SOUTH AMERICA. THE LOOT FROM THIS ONE SHIP MADE DRAKE AND HIS CREW RICH AND BROUGHT FABULOUS PROFITS TO DRAKE'S BACKERS, AMONG THEM QUEEN ELIZABETH.

England and Spain were at peace, Drake's actions, in his eyes, were legitimate acts of war.

After locking up her crew and sending his own men aboard *Cacafuego*, Drake ordered both ships to head out to sea, far from land. Next morning, after a hearty breakfast at which San Juan de Antón was guest of honor, he inspected the prize.

Even he was astonished at this floating treasure house. She carried eighty pounds of gold, thirteen chests of silver coins, twenty-six tons of silver bars, two large silver bowls, and what Chaplain Fletcher called other "trifles." As the loot was being hoisted aboard *Golden Hind*, a Spanish cabin boy renamed his ship *Cacaplata*—"Spitsilver." The English appreciated the joke. Once again, Drake's voyage was a success. Even if he captured nothing else, his backers would make a hefty profit.

Drake lined up his crew and handed out some of the booty. Each man put his mark on his share and returned it to the captain for safe-keeping until they reached home. Even the prisoners got something. Before setting them free with their ship, he gave each a gift in keeping with his rank. San Juan de Antón received two casks of tar, six hundred pounds of iron, a keg of gunpowder, a beautifully decorated musket from Germany, and a silver bowl with the Latin name *Franciscus Draques* engraved at the bottom. Ordinary sailors received forty pesos in cash, farm tools, knives, and clothing. Drake was a thief, but no one ever accused him of being a cheapskate.

These Spaniards and other former captives tell us more about life on the *Golden Hind* than any Englishman. Upon their release, they were questioned by the Inquisition to determine if they had been good Catholics in captivity and to learn about the enemy. To make sure they told the truth, the questioning went on for weeks, sometimes months. They knew that if they did not tell everything, or if they lied, the Inquisitors would find out. Each one had to repeat his story again and again, down to the smallest detail. Each story was written down word for word, then checked against earlier versions. If anything was changed, he had to explain why in great detail. If he could not, torture was used to "refresh" his memory.

All agreed that Drake ran a "tight ship." Don Francisco de Zarate, a nobleman who gave the best account, had been captured off the Mexican coast and watched him closely for two weeks. Drake, he says, occupied the large stern cabin. Fine furniture and carpets made the cabin feel like a room in a palace. Zarate continues:

> He is called Francisco Drac, and is a man of about 35 years of age,
> low of stature, with a fair beard, and is one of the greatest mariners that
> sails the seas, both as a navigator and as a commander. . . . He treats
> [his men] with affection, and they treat him with respect. He carries with
> him nine or ten [gentlemen]. These form a part of his council, which he
> calls together for even the most trivial matter, though he takes advice
> from no one. He enjoys hearing what they say and afterwards issues his
> orders. He has no favorite. . . . He is served on silver dishes with gold
> borders and gilded garlands. . . . He carries all possible dainties and
> perfumed waters. He said that many of these had been given him
> by the Queen. None of these gentlemen took a seat or covered his head
> before him, until he repeatedly urged them to do so. . . . He dines

and sups to the music of violins. . . . He shows [his men] great favor, but punishes the least fault. . . . I managed to ascertain whether [he] was well liked, and all said that they adored him.[19]

Drake conducted a religious service twice a day. The crew, all those not on duty, knelt while he read the prayers and led them in reciting a psalm. Sunday was the Lord's Day, a special time aboard ship. *Golden Hind* was decorated with flags and Chaplain Fletcher preached a sermon that might last two hours. At the end of the service, sailors danced a hornpipe, a lively jig played on an instrument resembling a clarinet. For their own safety, Spanish prisoners were sent below until the service ended. This was one time when ignorance was useful. Drake knew they would be questioned by the Inquisition and did not want them to get into trouble for attending a Protestant service.

Drake's "guests" reported that certain things stirred his anger. One involved his old lieutenant, John Oxenham, who had beaten him to the Pacific. In 1575, Oxenham led seventy men across the Isthmus of Panama. Once on the Pacific shore, he built a pinnace and set out after Spanish treasure ships. After capturing two fat prizes, the raiders were ambushed intheir camp by Spanish soldiers. All were executed as pirates, except Oxenham, who was handed over to the Inquisition in Lima. Drake learned of this while sailing up the Peruvian coast. Furious, he sent a warning to the viceroy: harm the Englishman and two thousand Spaniards would lose their heads. Oxenham was spared while Drake prowled offshore, only to be burned at the stake in 1581.

Nor had Drake forgotten San Juan de Ulua. He once asked a prisoner if a relative of Don Martín Enríquez or anything belonging to him was aboard a ship taken off the Mexican coast.

"No, sir," the prisoner replied.

"Well," said Drake, "it would give me greater joy to come across him than all the gold and silver of the Indies. You would see how the word of gentlemen should be kept."[20]

Fortunately, for Don Martín, they never met.

*C*apturing treasure was easy, compared to bringing it home safely. How should they return to England? There were three routes, none of them very appealing: doubling back through the Strait of Magellan, by way of the Northwest Passage, or across the Pacific and around the world.

The Strait of Magellan was out of the question. No one wanted to brave the storms and headwinds of the far south. Besides, the Spaniards were now on full alert and itching for a fight. The viceroy of Peru had sent a squadron to intercept the English at the entrance to the Strait. Its ships were not very large or well armed, but there was safety in numbers. If they attacked together, *Golden Hind* would be finished.

There was a different problem with the Northwest Passage, a channel joining the Atlantic and Pacific oceans along North America's arctic coast. Geographers were sure it existed, but no one would find it until 1854, and no ship would get through the pack ice until 1903.

Nevertheless, Drake decided to try his luck. For three months, from March to June in 1579, he sailed into the unknown. Once out of Mexican waters, he passed beyond the borders of Spanish settlement. Yet the further north he went, the further he seemed to be from his destination. Instead of the coastline trending eastward, it continued in a northwesterly direction. The weather turned bitter cold. Upon reaching Vancouver Island, the largest island on the West Coast of Canada, *Golden Hind* was enveloped in the "most vile, thick, and stinking fogs."[21] Drake had to turn back.

Golden Hind had sprung a leak and needed extensive repairs. On June 17, she anchored in a "convenient and fit harbor" on the California coast north of present-day San Francisco. Though the harbor's exact location is unknown, it was probably a bay on the Point Reyes Peninsula, since named Drake's Bay, a place with "white banks and cliffs which lie towards the sea."[22] This time Drake was on guard against unfriendly Indians. Armed sailors were sent ashore to secure the landing site. While they stood guard, others dug a trench and piled up the soil to form a wall faced with stones. When all was ready, tents were set up inside the "fort." *Golden Hind* could then be unloaded and careened on the beach.

Next morning, hundreds of Indians appeared. They were the Miwok, a tribe that lived by gathering wild fruits and hunting small animals. The arrival of strangers had startled them, and they came running with their weapons. But as they drew near, and saw the English clearly, they stopped in their tracks. Never having seen white people, they thought them gods from the sea; just as when Cortés landed in

AFTER RAIDING ALONG
THE WESTERN COAST
OF SOUTH AMERICA,
DRAKE LANDED IN
CALIFORNIA TO REFIT
THE GOLDEN HIND
BEFORE RETURNING
HOME THE LONG WAY—
BY SAILING COM-
PLETELY AROUND THE
WORLD. THIS PICTURE
SHOWS CALIFORNIA
INDIANS CROWNING
DRAKE THEIR "KING."

Mexico sixty years earlier, the Aztecs took his men for gods who traveled in "water houses." The Miwok threw down their weapons and began to worship the white "gods."

Drake was horrified; the very idea of man-worship was sinful to Christians. He tried to tell them, in sign language, that he was human, yet nothing could shake their belief.

The Miwok returned a few days later. News of the visitors had spread inland, bringing thousands down to the shore. A chief led the way, wearing a "crown" of colored feathers and carrying another in his hands. After a lengthy speech, of which the English understood not a word, he set the spare crown on Drake's head. Next he gave him a bag of dried tobacco, a sacred plant, because its fragrant smoke rose into the air to please the sky gods. When he finished, the women threw themselves on the ground and began to scratch themselves with their

fingernails. They tore their faces, their necks, and their breasts until the blood flowed. To calm them, Drake ordered his men to sing psalms. The Indians enjoyed the singing so much, that whenever it stopped, they cried *Gnaah*, "more."

Drake thought the chief had made him king of California. Perhaps. Perhaps not. Yet one thing is certain: Drake was a subject of Queen Elizabeth. He made that plain by engraving a brass plate with certain vital information. It contained the date of his arrival and a notice that he claimed the land for England. In 1936, a brass plate was found near San Quentin State Prison. How it got there no one knows. People still argue whether it is Drake's or a fake. The inscription reads:

BE IT KNOWN TO ALL MEN THESE PRESENTS, JUNE 17, 1579.
BY THE GRACE OF GOD AND IN THE NAME OF HER MAJESTY
QUEEN ELIZABETH OF ENGLAND AND HER SUCCESSORS
FOREVER I TAKE POSSESSION OF THIS KINGDOM WHOSE KING
AND PEOPLE FREELY RESIGN THEIR RIGHT AND TITLE IN THE
WHOLE LAND UNDER HER MAJESTY'S KEEPING NOW NAMED
BY ME AND TO BE KNOWN UNTO ALL MEN AS NOVA ALBION.

Francis Drake

Nova Albion—New Albion—refers to the white cliffs, like the white cliffs of Dover in England. If the plate is genuine, it is the first written record of the British Empire.

After stocking up on seal meat from offshore islands, the English sailed on July 23. The Miwok crowded the hilltops, waving good-bye as *Golden Hind* turned west to follow the sun. Her crew was going home the long way, sailing completely around the world.

Once clear of the coast, the crew saw no land for sixty-eight days. On September 30, they reached the Palaus, a group of coral islands northeast of the Philippines, which are named for King Philip II. Scores of canoes, graceful craft decorated with sea shells, came out to meet them. The dark-skinned oarsmen were totally naked, their ear-lobes stretched into weird shapes by heavy earrings and their teeth black from chewing betel, the seeds of a type of palm tree. At first they seemed eager to trade fish, fruit, and coconuts for cloth and other items. But no sooner did they come aboard, than they began to steal everything that wasn't nailed down. Ordered to leave, they showered *Golden Hind* with rocks kept in their canoes as weapons. It took a cannon shot, fired over their heads, to drive them away. Drake's men dubbed the place the "Islands of Thieves."

Golden Hind sailed on to Mindanao in the Philippines, stopping only for fresh water. Turning south, she continued for four hundred miles until the cone of a volcano rose in the distance. The volcano is on Ternate in the Moluccas; they had reached the fabled Spice Islands.

Columbus had set out not to find a New World, but to find a shortcut to these very islands. Ounce for ounce, spices were more valuable than gold. Spices had always served an important purpose. Before refrigeration, they were used to preserve meat and hide the taste of spoiled foods. Europeans also believed that using spices made for a long, healthy life. Spices were supposed to purify the blood, give nursing mothers milk, and prevent baldness. According to a leading medical authority: "Cinnamon warms, opens, and tones up the intestines. . . . It cures dropsy as well as defects and obstructions in the kidneys. Oil of cinnamon strengthens all organs: heart, stomach, liver, etc. . . . [Nutmegs] fortify the brain and sharpen the memory; they warm the stomach and expel winds. They give a clean breath, force the urine, stop diarrhea, and cure upset stomachs."[23]

Ternate was the richest of the Spice Islands. Sultan Babu, its ruler, had recently driven out the Portuguese. When Drake explained that he had been sent by a powerful European ruler, Babu agreed that their two nations should be friends. As a token of friendship, he allowed Drake to buy six tons of cloves, the most valuable of all spices, at cut-rate prices. In addition, Drake took aboard large quantities of pepper, ginger, rice, bananas, and sugar cane. *Golden Hind* sailed after five days, on November 9. She rode low in the water, her holds packed with treasure of every description. After a month's layover for repairs on a deserted island, she was ready for the final leg of the voyage.

The course lay through a maze of islands and channels that are today part of Indonesia. They were nearly through when, on January 8, 1580, the voyage nearly ended in disaster. *Golden Hind* struck the top of an undersea mountain and held fast. A wind from starboard kept the ship pinned to the reef. Each gust caused the ship to rock and made her timbers groan. If the wind continued from that direction, she would break up in a day or two, taking her crew to the bottom.

No one thought of money that night; it was a time of prayer and of making one's peace with God. At dawn, Drake decided to lighten ship by throwing overboard eight guns and three tons of cloves—"as much wealth as would break the heart of a miser to think on't."[24] Still she would not budge. And then it happened. After twenty hours, the wind shifted from starboard to port and *Golden Hind* slid into deep water.

The rest was routine. Sailing westward into the Indian Ocean, they rounded the Cape of Good Hope at the tip of Africa. The Dark Continent was on the *right*, which meant they were heading north, toward England.

On Monday, September 26, 1580, a cry came from one of the crow's nests: "Land ho!" There, rising in the distance, was the outline

GOLDEN HIND BEING TOWED INTO THE HARBOR OF TERNATE IN THE EAST INDIES BY THE SULTAN'S BARGES. DRAKE SAILED A FEW DAYS LATER, HAVING FILLED HIS SHIP'S HOLD WITH TONS OF SPICES WORTH THEIR WEIGHT IN GOLD IN EUROPE.

of Lizard Point. Soon everyone was on deck, pointing out the familiar landmarks.

Approaching Plymouth, *Golden Hind* fell in with some fishing boats. Drake leaned over the rail and called to the first man he saw: "Be the queen alive and well?" Upon hearing that she was, he breathed a sigh of relief.

So it ended, after two years, ten months and eleven days.

CHAPTER IV

A Fearful Man

Truly, Sir Francis Drake is a fearful man to the
King of Spain!
                —WILLIAM CECIL, *LORD BURGHLEY,* 1585

*N*ews of the *Cacafuego* reached Spain shortly after its capture. King Philip was outraged. Months before Drake's return, he instructed Don Bernardino de Mendoza, his ambassador in London, to demand the "pirate's" arrest the moment he set foot ashore. If the English refused, Mendoza was to threaten "grave consequences," a polite term for war.

The queen's advisors were split. On one side stood Lord Treasurer Burghley, the most powerful member of the Royal Council. A man of peace, Burghley thought it better to give back the treasure than risk war with such a powerful country. On the other side was Mr. Secretary Walsingham and Drake's backers. Convinced that Philip wanted war, they believed it would come regardless of what they did. Besides enriching themselves, keeping the treasure would make it harder for the king to pay his armies, forcing him to delay the final break.

Drake's most important backer, however, had already made up her mind. Her Majesty's anger with the Spanish king had not cooled since their meeting three years earlier. Time and again, Philip had shown hostile intentions. In 1579, he ordered Spanish "volunteers" to join an invasion force sent by the pope to Ireland. Although the invasion failed, it was a sign of things to come. Early in 1580, Spanish armies overran Portugal in a lightning campaign. Victory gave Philip not only

Portugal, but its overseas possessions, making the Spanish empire the largest in history. Worse for England, Philip also took the Portuguese battle fleet, instantly doubling his naval forces. As a Spanish historian noted: "The sun never set on the dominions of the King of Spain and at the slightest movement of that nation the whole earth trembled."[1]

Drake's return gave the queen a chance to show her displeasure. Having anchored at Plymouth, he stayed aboard ship, fearing what might happen if he came ashore. But when Elizabeth learned of his arrival, she ordered him to London. The order was stern in tone, but its message gentle: fear not—and bring samples.

Drake obeyed. He loaded two horses with the pick of the treasure and set out for the capital. The queen welcomed him as a devoted servant. His "samples," actually gifts, were more magnificent than she had imagined; they included sacks of gold coins, silver bowls and precious jewels, particularly three emeralds the size of her little finger and a cross studded with diamonds. But it was his adventures that really won her admiration. Their first meeting lasted six hours, during which he told her stories that would make science fiction seem dull. She could not get enough of them, or of him. In the days that followed, she saw him as often as nine times a day, a sure sign of favor. They would walk alone through the gardens of Richmond Palace, her hand resting on his arm, fascinated by his every word.

Drake was sent back to Plymouth to help register the treasure; every item had to be listed in an official inventory before being stored in the Tower of London. But the captain carried a secret letter with the queen's signature. Addressed to an official at Plymouth, it said the registration should not begin until Drake had been left alone with the treasure for a few days; that is, he would be allowed to take part of it without anybody looking. He could take £10,000 for himself and a similar amount for his crew. This was a drop in the bucket, compared to what remained. When everything was added up, the partners had a return of 4,700 percent on their investment. Her Majesty's share was more than her total yearly tax receipts. It allowed her to pay off the whole of her foreign debt and freed her from the need to borrow for a whole year.

Bernardino de Mendoza was at his wit's end. He begged. He pleaded. He demanded. But each time he opened his mouth, Her Majesty turned away: she refused to listen until his master apologized for the Irish invasion. The ambassador finally lost his temper. If she would not listen to his words, he snapped, perhaps she would listen to

Spanish guns. The queen would not be bullied. "If you talk to me like that," she said calmly, her voice falling to a whisper, "I will put you in a place where you cannot talk at all."[2] Mendoza bowed deeply and backed out of the royal presence.

Elizabeth had the last word. She ordered *Golden Hind* moved to Deptford and knighted its captain. "My deare pyrat," as she called him, would be known from then on as Sir Francis Drake.

The country went wild with joy. Poets sang the praises of the first Englishman to circumnavigate the globe. Preachers compared his victories against mighty Spain to David's against Goliath. The common people loved him as one of their own. To them, he was the poor boy who had made good, a true hero. "The people generally applauded his wonderful adventures and rich prizes," noted the historian John Stow. "His name and fame became admirable in all places, the people swarming daily in the streets to behold him, swearing hatred to all that misliked him."[3]

His fame spread beyond England. The King of Denmark, a Protestant, named his best warship *Drake*. Even enemies admired his courage. In Catholic Italy, one could buy his picture with the inscription, *Il Drago, gran corsaro Inglese:* "Drake, the great English corsair."

Sir Francis enjoyed his fame and wealth. He bought a mansion, Buckland Abbey, a few miles north of Plymouth. In Plymouth itself, he bought enough property to make him the town's third largest landlord, next to Hawkins and the town council itself. He became mayor of Plymouth in 1581 and a member of Parliament in 1583, the year his wife, Mary, died. Nothing is known of her except that she was his wife and the daughter of a seaman. Two years later, he married Elizabeth Sydenham, the daughter of a knight. Both marriages remained childless. Nevertheless, Drake was a warm person who loved children. Robert Hayman, a future governor of Newfoundland, recalled their

THE VOYAGE OF CIRCUMNAVIGATION MADE FRANCIS DRAKE RICH AND FAMOUS, AND EARNED HIM A TITLE OF NOBILITY. SOON AFTER HIS RETURN, HE MARRIED ELIZABETH SYDENHAM, HIS SECOND WIFE. THE COUPLE HAD NO CHILDREN.

meeting in a poem, "Of the Great and Famous, Ever to be Honored Knight, Sir Francis Drake, and of my Little, Little Self." One day, Drake stopped outside the Hayman home:

> *This man when I was little, I did meet,*
> *As he walked up [the] long street.*
> *He asked me whose I was. I answered him.*
> *He asked if his good friend was within.*
> *A fair red orange in his hand he had.*
> *He gave it me, whereof I was right glad,*
> *Takes and kissed me, and prays, 'God bless my boy.'*
> *Which I record with comfort to this day.*[4]

Still there were reminders that the happy times ashore could not last long. The Spanish king had sworn vengeance and was making his plans. Philip II was a key figure in Drake's story, and we must now get to know him better.

Born in 1527, Philip II came to the throne at the age of twenty-nine. He was short and slim, with blue eyes, brown hair and beard, thick lips, and a large jaw. In private life, he was a good man, decent, caring and generous. A devoted father, he enjoyed helping his little daughters, Isabella and Catherine, with their lessons. During tours around his kingdom, he frequently wrote them of his love and to ask how things were going at home. He questioned them about everything: "Do the clocks keep time at San Lorenzo? How much have you grown since I saw you last? Let me have the measurements exactly?"[5] In addition, he was kind to the poor and tried to be just, even at his own expense. He once told a judge that when in doubt, the verdict must always go against the king. The people should always have the benefit of the doubt.

Philip believed in the Divine Right of Kings, that is, that God created monarchy and gave each ruler his (or her) throne. Kingship was a heavy responsibility, heavier than that borne by any of his subjects. If he had power and wealth, it was only to be used for the welfare of the Spanish people. Not that he felt bound to consider their wishes, much less fear their disapproval. The people could not hold him accountable for his actions; that would be democracy, a dangerous idea in the six-teenth century. A king must answer to a higher power. If he ruled well, God would reward him with eternal life in heaven. But if he failed, or became a tyrant, God would reward him differently; he would burn in hell throughout eternity.

"Being a king," he said, "is none other than a form of slavery which carries with it a crown."[6] Night after night, until the wee hours, he sat at his desk in San Lorenzo de Escorial. Part palace, part monastery, the Escorial is located in the mountains north of Madrid. The king built it in honor of Saint Lawrence, his favorite saint, who had been burned to death on a gridiron. Designed as an upright gridiron, the Escorial's four towers

KING PHILIP II RULED SPAIN'S VAST EMPIRE FROM HIS STUDY IN THE ESCORIL. A KIND, GENTLE MAN IN HIS EVERYDAY LIFE, PHILIP BELIEVED THAT GOD HAD CHOSEN HIM TO DEFEND CATHOLICISM AT ANY COST. TO THAT END, HE SUPPORTED THE SPANISH INQUISITION AND LAUNCHED THE "INVINCIBLE ARMADA" AGAINST ENGLAND.

represent the legs. Though it has hundreds of large rooms, the ruler of half the world lived alone in a cell twelve feet square. That cell, and not Madrid, was Spain's true capital. There the king read all government papers, correcting the spelling and making notes in the margins on everything from a battle plan to the type of bugs that flew around an ambassador's reading lamp. Rather than dictate to a secretary, Philip wrote important documents himself, signing them *Yo el Rey*, "I, The King."

A deeply religious man, Philip's chief concerns were the souls of his people and the good of the Catholic church; indeed, they were one and the same. In this, he was very different from Queen Elizabeth, who was fond of saying: "I do not wish to make windows into men's souls." By this she meant that people could worship God however they pleased, so long as they were loyal subjects and obeyed the law. Philip, however, believed it his sacred duty to help the church help his subjects get to heaven.

This could not happen unless "false beliefs" were crushed and "false prophets" silenced. Gentle as he was in private life, Philip supported the Inquisition wholeheartedly. Torture was fine, he believed, so long as it unmasked heretics. Killing heretics was like amputating a diseased limb: painful, to be sure, but necessary to save the rest of the body. Because heretics threatened to poison others' minds, he burned them by the hundreds. He did so with determination, even joy. As one victim, a nobleman, was being led to execution, he shouted to the king: "How can you let me burn?" Philip answered: "If my son were as wicked as you I would carry the wood to burn him myself."[7]

We have no reason to doubt the king's sincerity. For him, anything was justified if it supported and furthered the "true religion." There was no need, he insisted, to keep faith with "God's enemies." He lied for the "glory of God." He favored (and ordered) the assassination of fellow rulers, certain that he was doing "God's work." Philip's nature was that of the fanatic.

By the 1580s, Spain and England were on a collision course. Philip was on the march everywhere. In France, his money helped start another civil war between Protestants and Catholics. In the Netherlands, one of his agents murdered William of Orange, the Dutch resistance leader. In England, Bernardino de Mendoza was expelled for his role in a plot to assassinate Queen Elizabeth. Relations seemed to improve when Philip asked England to send grain to avoid starvation in northern Spain, where the crops had failed. The grain ships went, but they were not received as friends. In May 1585, Philip seized them all—all, that is, except the *Primrose*, whose crew beat off the attackers and brought the news to England.

Queen Elizabeth struck back. For starters, she sent a small army to aid the Dutch rebels. Next, she invited the merchants who'd lost their ships to become privateers. Privateers were not part of the navy, but licensed thieves who waged "private war." Privateering is outlawed today, but for centuries governments issued "letters of marque and reprisal" allowing citizens who had been wronged by a foreign power to take revenge by seizing its shipping. Finally, in September, she unleashed Sir Francis Drake. No longer was he a corsair whom she could disavow whenever she pleased. Now he was her trusted servant, operating under a royal commission.

*D*rake sailed in September with two Royal Navy ships, twenty-three privateering vessels and 2,300 men, half of them soldiers. Among the ships was the *Primrose*, her crew thirsting for revenge. They were led by a first-class fighting team. Drake's second-in-command was Martin Frobisher, a hot-tempered seaman who lived for loot. The soldiers were led by Christopher Carleill, a veteran of the Low Countries and Ireland. Richard Hawkins, John's son, represented his family's interests. Drake's cousin had not forgotten San Juan de Ulua either.

Their mission was to free the English ships, then strike at Philip's American colonies. If possible, they were to seize the annual treasure fleet which was returning to Spain. Failing that, they would capture and loot the colonial ports themselves. These were violent acts; most people nowadays would call them acts of war. Not Queen Elizabeth. War, to her, meant taking another country's home territory. This did not include its colonies, much less its ships on the high seas. Drake's campaign, like his raid into the Pacific, was to be a punishment for the past and a warning for the future. But it was not war.

Drake's first stop was the port of Vigo in northwestern Spain. The fleet swept into the harbor without warning, turned broadside to the city, and ran out its guns. Drake sent a messenger ashore with two demands for the governor. If their countries were still at peace, the captured grain ships must be freed at once and his fleet resupplied as a sign of goodwill. If they were at war, Drake would give him a bellyful. The governor said His Majesty had changed his mind a week ago; the ships had already been released. The English could buy all the supplies they wanted.

Without knowing it, the governor had won a major victory— Spain's last in 1585. Several days were needed to gather and load the supplies. The delay was long enough for a storm to trap the fleet in Vigo harbor. By the time it passed, the treasure fleet had arrived safely at another port. Drake missed the prize by less than twelve hours!

He went on to the Cape Verde Islands, a Portuguese colony off the West African coast. On November 16, the fleet dropped anchor at Santiago, the chief town. That night, Sir Francis tried a tactic he would use many times in the future. While some ships held the defenders' attention, others put Carleill's troops ashore at an unguarded spot several miles away. Advancing unobserved, at dawn the soldiers reached a hill overlooking the town. Below, were its main land-side defenses, a row of fifty loaded cannons.

November 17 was the twenty-seventh anniversary of Her Majesty's coronation, considered a lucky day in England. And so it was again. The Spanish gunners, taken by surprise, deserted their post without firing a shot. Carleill decided to celebrate in style. He walked along the row of guns, firing one after another. Drake understood and replied in kind. Before long, every gun in the fleet had taken up the salute.

Attacked by land and sea, Santiago's defenders quickly surrendered. The English occupied the town for ten days. Though there was plenty of food, they found no gold or silver. They burned the place to the ground.

The fleet crossed the Atlantic, bound for Santo Domingo on the southern coast of Hispaniola. Founded in 1496, it was the first permanent European settlement in the New World, and as the capital of the West Indies, it was strongly defended. In addition to a squadron of small warships, the harbor had a heavy iron chain across its entrance and a fort, bristling with guns, on a hillside above. By land, the town was protected by stone walls manned by a large garrison. It would be suicide to attack head-on. If the town was to be taken at all, it had to be taken by surprise.

Sir Francis planned a repeat of the Santiago attack, but with one difference: the Cimaroon. Hispaniola, like Panama, had thousands of escaped slaves who hated their former masters. These Cimaroon lived in the mountains behind Santo Domingo. The town walls had been built not to ward off attacks by whites, but to keep the blacks at a safe distance. It didn't work. The Cimaroon struck often and hard. Time and again, the governor sent soldiers into the mountains, only to have them disappear. It was as if the mountain spirits had swallowed them, bones and all.

Some of Drake's officers had been with him in Panama and knew how he operated. One night, they made contact with the Cimaroon. The blacks already knew about their adventure; news traveled quickly from the mainland to the islands. The officers explained that the beach they intended to land on was overlooked by guardhouses. No need to say more; the Cimaroon knew the rest and promised to do their part.

On New Year's Eve, 1586, Carleill came ashore with a thousand men. All was quiet. An hour earlier, the guards had been at their posts.

CARLEILL'S MEN CAME ASHORE BELOW THE CITY AND JOINED CIMAROONS TO ATTACK SANTO DOMINGO, WHILE DRAKE'S FLEET KEPT THE PORT DEFENSES OCCUPIED.

They were making their rounds, when suddenly black hands reached out of the darkness. A few quick knife thrusts and the guards lay in pools of blood. Nothing stood between the troops and their objective.

At dawn, the fleet suddenly appeared off Santo Domingo. As longboats were being lowered, the garrison marched out to meet the expected attack. Flags flying and trumpets blaring, they took up positions on the beach west of the city.

That was exactly what Drake wanted. Lowering the longboats was merely a "demonstration," a trick to get the defenders to look the wrong way. While they faced seaward, Carleill hit them from behind. Caught between the fleet's guns and the infantry's muskets, the Spaniards ran for the city gates, the attackers close behind. No one aboard the ships knew what was happening. They could hear shots and see smoke rising from the city, but it was impossible to tell who had the upper hand. At last, a flag was unfurled on top of a building. It was the cross of St. George. "Thus," wrote an officer, "the Spaniards gave us the town for a New Year's gift."[8]

Drake decided to hold Santo Domingo for a million ducats in ransom. The Spanish authorities were shocked. They expected to pay ransom (as was the custom of the time), but such an amount was impossible, they said. He must settle for less. How much less was the subject of a hot debate.

Day after day, both sides exchanged messages with their latest offer. One day, Sir Francis sent a black youngster on such an errand. We do not know his identity or why he was chosen. He may have been a Cimaroon, or a slave freed after the city's capture. In any case, a Spanish officer was insulted that such a person should be entrusted with an important message. As he approached, the officer ran him through with a spear. The youngster managed to crawl back to camp, dying at his commander's feet.

Drake was so angry that his emotions got the best of him. Among his prisoners were several Catholic priests, men innocent of any crime. He ordered two priests to be hung on the spot where the youngster died. A third priest was sent to the governor with a message: two priests would be hanged at the same hour each day until the murderer was handed over.

Next morning, the Spaniards did as they were told. Drake, however, was not satisfied. To save the priests' lives, he demanded that the

Spaniards execute the murderer themselves. Both sides assembled their troops to watch the execution. It was the first, and only, time Drake mistreated prisoners.

The Spaniards continued haggling over the ransom. His patience gone, Sir Francis raised the stakes. First he burned a chapel north of town. When that did not open their purses, he ordered Santo Domingo to be leveled brick by brick. The work was hard, but his men enjoyed it. Churches were a special target. "We burned all their images of wood," says *Primrose's* log, "brake and destroyed all their fairest work within the churches, and we had in the town much [silver] plate, money and pearls hidden in wells and other places."[9] Soon a third of the town lay in ruins and the Spanish ships were sunk in the harbor. At last Drake realized his demands were too high. Instead of a million ducats, he accepted a ransom of 25,000 for the rest of the city. On February 1, he sailed for the Spanish Main.

Spaniards had always thought of Santo Domingo as the jewel of their empire. Its ruin, therefore, was a terrific blow to national pride. Only God could have allowed such a calamity to happen. "This thing," wrote the deputy governor, "must have had Divine sanction, as punishment for the people's sins."[10] A priest named Father Pedro agreed: it was God's retribution for their crimes against the Indians. In Spain itself, Drake's action was seen as a personal insult to Philip II. "It was such a cooling to King Philip," an official noted, "as never happened to him since he was King of Spain."[11]

Cartagena was the fleet's next objective. The city was built at the base of a long peninsula joined to the mainland by a bridge on one side and a sliver of land on the other. Its inner (main) harbor was separated from the outer harbor by a channel, wide as two ships, guarded by a fort. The peninsula itself was defended by a line of trenches across the narrowest part of the base. To prevent a landing from the sea, thousands of poisoned stakes were planted along the shore.

On February 9, Drake anchored a mile from the entrance to the inner harbor. His tactics were by then routine. As Frobisher bombarded the fort, Carleill would lead his troops along the shore. Fortunately, two black fishermen warned them about the poisoned stakes. At sundown, the soldiers began to move. But instead of marching on dry land, they went up to their waists through the wash of the surf. Not only did they avoid the stakes, they came up on the unprotected flank, or side, of the channel.

CARTAGENA,
CAPITAL OF THE
SPANISH MAIN,
AS IT APPEARED AT
THE TIME OF
ITS CAPTURE BY
SIR FRANCIS DRAKE.

Cartagena's defenders were a mixed lot. Soldiers and civilian volunteers stood beside priests armed with swords and pikes. Not everyone, however, was so warlike. Many wealthy people had fled with their money. One fellow, quite brave with his mouth, sneaked away dressed as a woman. Even so, the Spaniards were no pushover. After a fierce fight, in which thirty Englishmen were killed, they surrendered.

Having secured the city, Drake went to the governor's office. There, on the desk, he found a letter from Philip II referring to him as a *corsario*. "No," he snapped. He was no pirate, but an officer in Her Majesty's service, and God help anyone who said differently. On the second day, to show his displeasure, he allowed his men to loot the city and keep whatever they found. That is all they had to hear.

Churches were stripped, warehouses emptied, and private homes searched from top to bottom. Slaves helped by revealing where their masters' valuables were hidden.

Sir Francis demanded six hundred thousand ducats in ransom, only to have the city fathers plead poverty. That was the last straw. If they refused to pay, he promised to flatten their city. He meant what he said; let them ask the citizens of Santo Domingo.

It was easy to sink every ship in the harbor and blow up the fort with kegs of gunpowder. Nevertheless, the work of destruction went slowly. The city was built of stone, and the weather was hot and steamy. Clouds of mosquitoes rose from the marshes, causing an epidemic of malaria and yellow fever. Drake was forced to lower his demand to 110,000 ducats, which the city fathers agreed to pay. At the end of March, after a six-week stay, he put to sea.

A Spanish "rescue" fleet reached Cartagena a few days later, only to be greeted by jeers and catcalls. The fleet, people said, was "an old ass laden with lances lacking steel heads"—the Spanish version of "too little too late." Once the richest city of the Spanish Main, Cartagena had become an empty shell. According to an official report: "The damage done by this corsair amounts to more than 400,000 ducats. . . . In burning and looting it the English have left this city so completely destroyed and desolate that its present condition deserves the deepest pity."[12]

Panama City was to have been Drake's next target. But with disease ravaging the ships, he decided to set a course for home. At Cuba, the English landed to take on fresh water. To speed the work, their commander plunged into the surf up to his shoulders, fully dressed, carrying a water barrel.

From there Drake sailed into the opening chapter of North American history. On May 27, he came to St. Augustine, Florida, Spain's first colony in what was to become the United States. He burned it to ashes. Continuing up the coast, on June 9 he reached Roanoke Island off North Carolina. There he found Ralph Lane in command of one hundred and five men, the first English settlers in North America. Having arrived only nine months before, they were already fed up with this "horrid wilderness." Sir Francis took them aboard and set sail; it would be another twenty-one years before the English set up a permanent colony in Virginia, named for the Virgin Queen.

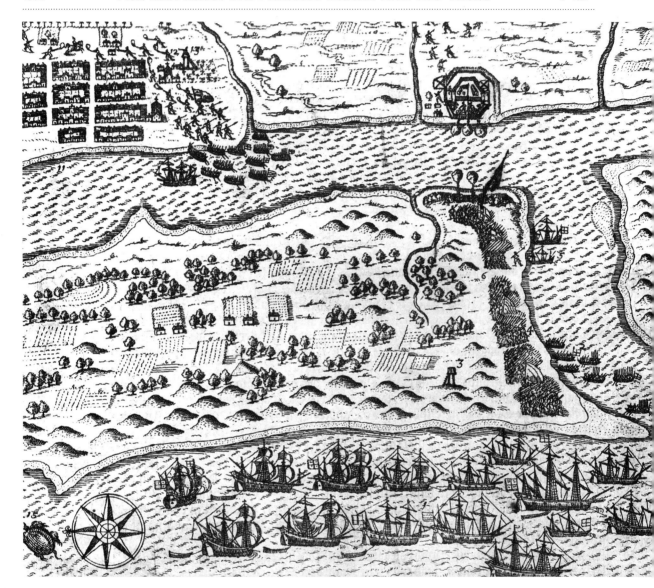

DRAKE BURNED ST. AUGUSTINE, SPAIN'S FIRST COLONY IN WHAT WAS TO BECOME THE UNITED STATES.

Drake reached Plymouth on July 28, 1586. The voyage had claimed the lives of 750 men, three quarters of them victims of disease. No one seemed troubled by the loss except, perhaps, the victims' families. The loot was officially valued to £105,000; the sailors and soldiers actually brought in more, which they never declared or paid taxes on.

Queen Elizabeth could say whatever she wished, but this was war. Philip II certainly thought so. One night, he sat alone in his room in the Escorial. On his desk lay a pile of reports from the New World. His eyes burned and his head ached. He had read enough.

Taking up a pen, he wrote a long letter to Don Alvaro de Bazan, Marquis of Santa Cruz. At 71, Santa Cruz was Spain's leading admiral. Known as the "Never Defeated," in 1571 he had led his fleet to victory at Lepanto, an epic battle that broke the naval power of Turkey in the Mediterranean Sea. The king now gave him the assignment of a lifetime. He must carry out history's greatest naval operation: the invasion and conquest of England. Officially named the Enterprise of England, most people called it simply the Spanish Armada.

Santa Cruz set to work with his usual energy. Before long, men, ships, and supplies were pouring into the staging areas, the ports of Cadiz, Spain, and Lisbon, Portugal. Meanwhile, Mr. Secretary Walsingham's "ears" were as keen as ever. His spies reported the buildup as soon as it began.

The queen asked her "deare pyrat's" advice. Drake gave it freely: there was no time to lose. Hit first! Hit fast! Hit hard! Clearly, the Armada could not be stopped by attacks in the New World. The attacks must be aimed at Spain itself. And he was just the man to lead them.

Elizabeth agreed, giving him the rank of Her Majesty's Admiral-at the-Seas. This was more than a high-sounding title. It was a bold step, bolder even than making him a knight. For she was announcing to the world that Sir Francis Drake was her man, acting under her direct orders.

*T*he admiral sailed from Plymouth on April 2, 1587, with 2,200 men aboard twenty-three ships and seven pinnaces. The four largest vessels were Royal Navy men-of-war of a type known as the galleon: *Elizabeth Bonaventure* (Drake's flagship), *Dreadnought*, *Rainbow*, and *Golden Lion*. Swift and well armed, these were the fleet's heavy hitters. Their sisters were privateers sailing for patriotism and profit.

Drake's instructions were to keep the Spaniards away from England at all costs. If they were already at sea, he must find them and fight them. If not, he was to cut off their supplies. Most importantly, he was ordered, in writing, "to distress the ships within the havens themselves." Translation: he could invade Philip's kingdom with ships and soldiers. Even by the Queen's own definition, that was war. In the language of the nuclear age, Drake was launching a "first strike."

As the fleet weighed anchor, Drake wrote Walsingham: "The wind commands me away. Our ship is under sail. God grant we may so live in His fear as the enemy may have cause to say that God fights for Her Majesty. . . . Haste!"[13] This was no boast; it came from the man's very soul. Now, more than ever, Drake believed in himself and in his mission. Serving England by fighting Spain was actually serving God.

His destination was Cadiz, the Spanish navy's home port. The city is built on an island at the end of a peninsula four miles long. Two harbors lie between the peninsula and the mainland, both well protected. Rocks and sandbars turn the approaches to the outer harbor into an obstacle course. Once inside, a ship must enter a narrow channel, guarded by cannons, before reaching the inner harbor, where a dozen war galleys were on permanent station.

A galley was 120 feet long, and 15 feet wide, and powered by 222 rowers chained three or four to an oar. It was armed with a long bronze beak in its bow and five forward-firing guns; the banks of oars prevented guns from being mounted broadside. Highly maneuverable in calm seas, the galley's basic tactic was to rush an enemy and ram with its beak. Musketeers crowded on its upper deck stood ready to pick off enemy sailors and board the enemy ship after ramming. The battle of Lepanto had been fought by two huge galley fleets.

On April 29, the people of Cadiz felt safe. The leading citizens were in the main square, laughing at the antics of a troupe of traveling comedians. Elsewhere, a crowd cheered as an acrobat performed amazing stunts. About four o'clock in the afternoon, there was a commotion at the fringes of the crowd. *"Inglés! Inglés!,"* people shouted. "The English! The English!" Ships sailing under the Cross of St. George were off the coast and coming fast.

Panic swept the city. The mayor, expecting the raiders to land at any moment, ordered women and children to take shelter in a castle standing at the end of a long, narrow street. The castle's commander, however, wanted nothing to do with civilians at such a time; he shut the gates and prepared for battle. It was the worst thing he could have done. Blocked by the gates in front and pushed by crowds from behind, nearly a hundred people were crushed to death. In this way, more died before the first shot was fired than during the battle that followed.

There was also panic in the outer harbor, crowded with merchant ships riding at anchor. What followed can only be compared to a pack of wolves pouncing on a herd of sheep. The Spaniards cut their anchor cables and scrambled for safety. The lucky vessels made it to the inner harbor. The unlucky vessels were chased down and boarded by the

English crews. Anyone who expected the galleys to protect the town was quickly disappointed. The galley, as Drake proved, was no match for heavy sailing ships with broadside guns.

Since galleys could only fire straight ahead, they came on line abreast, one beside the other. They were an impressive sight, moving in formation, their oars rhythmically dipping and flashing in the sun. Drake dealt with them by inventing a new tactic. We do not know how he got the idea, or even if it was his own. What we do know is that he formed his galleons into line ahead; that is, one behind the other. Gradually, the galleons pulled ahead of the galleys, passing before them at right angles. This "crossing the T" allowed their broadsides to rake the enemy from bow to stern. Nearly every shot hit something, turning the galleys into a bloody shambles. Musketeers were literally blown away. Horribly mangled rowers screamed and died where they sat, chained to their oars. A galley ran aground in flames. Nine others, riddled with cannon balls and leaking, took shelter behind a reef. Two of them were in sinking condition and had to be towed ashore.

Meanwhile, the privateers swept the outer harbor clean. Every Spanish ship was looted and burned. Explosions split the air as flames reached kegs of gunpowder. Now and then, if the wind was right, the crackling and hissing of burning timbers could be heard ashore.

That night was unlike any Cadiz had ever known. Thousands jammed the roads out of town, desperate to escape before those "horrible fiends," the *Inglés*, landed. As they trudged along, they passed reinforcements marching into the city. Civilians and soldiers made their way by the glare of burning ships. Some said the flames made the city bright as day.

Drake was not satisfied. From the distance he could see a forest of masts in the inner harbor. He had learned from captives that a magnificent new galleon was anchored close to the shore. The personal property of the Marquis of Santa Cruz, she had come to Cadiz to be fitted with guns. When fully armed, she would take her place as flagship of the invasion fleet. She was a fine target, too good to pass up.

To reach her, however, Drake's galleons would have to sail close to the shore batteries. Rather than risk them, he decided to let smaller craft do the job. At daybreak, he led the pinnaces through the channel. Spanish guns banged away, and there were some near misses, but the pinnaces came through without a scratch. Before long, Englishmen were clambering aboard Santa Cruz's galleon. After a nasty little fight, they tossed the crew overboard and set the ship ablaze. Most of the other ships received similar treatment. One was loaded with food for the fleet at Lisbon; another had a cargo of rope, tar, and canvas. These were towed away. By the time Drake returned to *Elizabeth Bonaventure*, a pall of smoke hovered over the inner harbor. It was time to leave.

And then the wind dropped. The victorious fleet was stranded in the outer harbor. Once again the galleys moved to the attack. This time they were in their element, being able to bear in for the kill while the English enemy lay helpless—or so their captains thought. Once again Drake reached into his bag of tricks. As soon as he saw the galleys, he sent out longboats to haul on the galleons' bow cables. It worked like a charm. Each time the galleys approached, the boat crews pulled on their oars, swinging the larger vessels by the bow cables in a wide arc. No matter how the galleys dodged and circled, they could not avoid those murderous broadsides.

The galleys retreated, returning a few hours later with fireships on the ends of *their* cables. After being towed into position, the fireships were ignited and set adrift. The English were ready. The moment they caught fire, sailors in longboats pushed them aside with poles. Drake was thrilled. "The Spaniards," he cried, "are doing our work for us by burning their own ships."[14] Men shouted the joke from *Elizabeth Bonaventure* to a nearby ship, and its crew passed it along. Everyone in the fleet had a good laugh at the enemy's expense.

About midnight, a land breeze whipped across the harbor. The fleet stood out to sea with flags flying and guns roaring. They had reason to celebrate. Not one Englishman had been killed or seriously wounded in two days of fighting. The Spaniards admitted losing twenty-four ships at Cadiz; Drake claimed thirty-seven. Back at the Escorial, King Philip was not quibbling over numbers. "The loss," he said after reading the reports, "was not very great, but the daring of the attempt was very great indeed."[15]

Drake moved on to Cape St. Vincent on the Portuguese coast. Located 150 miles west of Cadiz, it lay across the Spanish navy's chief supply line. All ships coming from the Mediterranean to Lisbon had to sail around it. And Lisbon was to be the Armada's jump-off point. Once preparations were complete, its ships were to assemble there for the move into the English Channel. By seizing this key point, Drake could cut the enemy supply line and keep the Armada off balance.

The Cape was defended by Sagres Castle. Built atop a steep cliff, it commanded the best harbor with its guns. On May 5, Drake led his men up the side of the cliff. Once on top, his musketeers pinned down the defenders while sailors piled brush against the wooden gate and set it on fire. The admiral worked alongside the assault party, exposing himself to the same dangers. After two hours, with the gate in ruins and English bullets striking home, the garrison surrendered. Drake allowed them to leave with all their baggage, except their weapons. The castle was then blown up and its guns thrown off the cliff, to be collected by the men below. Guns had no nationality; they could serve either side.

Drake turned the Cape into an attack base. While some ships were careened for repairs, others cruised along the coast. For the next week, nothing of military value escaped the torch. Englishmen ravaged Portugal's tuna industry, a major source of food for the Armada. Not only did they sink fishing boats, they cut fishing nets and burned

LISBON, PORTUGAL'S CAPITAL AND GREATEST SEAPORT, AS DRAKE MUST HAVE SEEN IT.

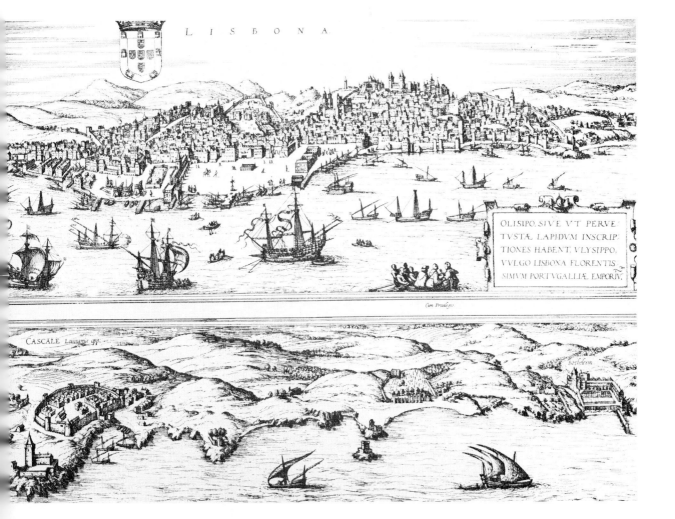

fishing villages. Scores of supply ships were also sent to the bottom, many of them loaded with cooperage; that is, hoops and staves for making barrels. These humble items were more precious than gold at sea. Everything sailors ate and drank came in barrels. A barrel had to be made of seasoned wood, usually oak. If the wood was not properly dried, the barrel would shrink, letting in air and spoiling the contents. By burning hundreds of tons of fine cooperage, Drake's men hurt the Armada more than all the ships lost at Cadiz.

Drake reached Lisbon on May 10, anchoring in Cascaes Bay at the mouth of the Tagus River. Beyond, he could see St. Julian's Tower, Santa Cruz's headquarters, and the forts that lined the way to the Portuguese capital. In the harbor were thirty big ships of all types and seven galleys. The marquis would have jumped at the chance to fight, except that his fleet wasn't ready for combat. The galleys *were* ready, but their captains already knew about Cadiz and were terrified of English broadsides.

If one admiral could not come out, the other dared not go in after him. Lisbon's defenses were too strong, and Drake had no pilots to guide him through the tricky passage upriver. He sailed back and forth across Cascaes Bay, challenging Santa Cruz to fight like a man. The marquis brushed that aside as the bellowing of braggart; he had already proven his manhood in more battles than Drake had years. Even when Drake threatened to sell Spanish prisoners to the Turks as slaves, he swallowed his anger and stayed put. There was nothing else to do but weigh anchor and return to Cape St. Vincent.

Letters signed *Yo el Rey* poured from the tiny room in the Escorial. Troops were sent to reinforce coastal cities. Orders came for Santa Cruz to put to sea as quickly as possible. It was useless. On May 22, a Spanish patrol boat darted past Drake's anchorage below Sagres Castle. Empty! The English had vanished as suddenly as they had come.

Not that they were really gone. Somehow Drake had learned that a carrack was due back from the Far East any day. The *San Felipe* was King Philip's personal property. She had spent the winter in the Portuguese colony of Mozambique, East Africa, and was on the last leg of a two-year voyage. She had already rounded the "bulge" of Africa and was approaching the Azores, a group of islands about eight hundred miles off the coast of Portugal. A few days more, and she would be home.

On June 9, a galleon and several pinnaces slid over the horizon, making way at top speed. The oceans were vast, voyages long and lonely. Seamen had a natural curiosity about any vessel they met.

It was good to "speak" to another ship, to share the latest news. The trouble came when you found that curiosity had brought you within striking distance of foreign enemies or pirates. *San Felipe*'s crew, however, had nothing to fear. In those waters, the stranger could only be a friend.

San Felipe dipped her colors in greeting. The stranger flew no flag. That should have alerted the Spanish captain; a favorite pirate trick was to fly the flag of a friendly nation, or none at all, and "show his true colors" just before attacking.

The stranger was none other than *Elizabeth Bonaventure*. As she drew near, she ran out her guns and ran up the Cross of St. George. "We, knowing what she was" an eyewitness recalled, "would put out no flag until we were within shot of her, when we hanged out flags, streamers, and pendants, that she might be out of doubt what we were. Which done, we hailed her with cannon-shot; and having shot her through divers times, she shot at us. . . . Then we began to ply her hotly, our flyboat and one of our pinnaces lying [across her bows], at whom she shot and threw fireworks, but did them no hurt, for her [guns] lay so high over them [that they could not be pointed down at a sharp angle]. Then she seeing us ready to lay her aboard . . . six of her men being dead and divers others sore hurt, they yielded unto us."[16]

San Felipe was truly a royal ship, worth a king's ransom. A partial list of her cargo includes: 780 bundles of Chinese silk, 6,573 pieces of calico cloth, a chest of jewels, 330 tons of spices and 420 bales of indigo, a valuable blue dye. She also carried four hundred Negroes bound for the slave markets of Portugal and Spain. Not only did Drake set them free, he gave them a small boat to go wherever they pleased. *San Felipe*'s passengers and crew were put aboard a merchant vessel with their baggage and sent to the Azores. Their ship, with an English prize crew, was brought home to Plymouth, arriving on June 26, 1587.

Drake could afford to be generous. *San Felipe* was valued at £114,000, making her the richest prize ever taken up to that time. The expedition's backers did very well indeed. Queen Elizabeth received £46,672 for the loan of her four galleons. Drake earned £18,235 for less than three months' work. His share could have bought plenty of fighting power. A galleon the size of his flagship cost £2,600 to build. Had Drake wished, he could have built seven *Elizabeth Bonaventure* and formed his own private navy.

Sir Francis Drake had become Spain's most feared enemy. Spaniards called him *El Draque*: "the Dragon." Crews jumped ship rather than sail if rumor had it that he had put to sea. Mothers used his name to frighten disobedient children; unless they behaved, the Dragon would swallow them headfirst. In the ports of Spain and the New World, educated men whispered about his magic mirror (some said crystal ball), which showed the location of every vessel on the high seas. He had sold his soul to the devil for that mirror, they said. He was a witch, and would be burned alive if he ever fell into the hands of the Inquisition.

Drake said he had "singed the King of Spain's beard." That was not a boast, but a warning. He had hurt the enemy, but the wound was not mortal. He had delayed the Armada until the following year and bought his country some more time. Those extra months were precious and could not be wasted. "Prepare in England strongly, and most by sea," he wrote Walsingham. The Armada was coming!

CHAPTER V

The Spanish Armada

*In the yeare 1588 there sailed from Spain the
greatest Navy that ever swam upon the sea.*
—SIR FRANCIS BACON

As the year 1588 opened, astrologers had reason to worry about
the future. Wherever they turned, they saw evil omens. The Dutch
had recently plucked a two-headed whale from the North Sea. From
Germany came reports of snakes swallowing their own tails and frogs
falling from the sky. Elsewhere, the earth trembled and black shadows
were seen to fall across the face of the moon. "These are the signs pre-
ceding the end of the world," a Protestant minister declared. "Satan is
roaring like a lion and the world is going mad."

Englishmen saw Philip II as Satan, and he was madder than ever. In
the months following Drake's raid, His Majesty devoted almost every
waking hour to the Armada. He wrote orders, appointed officers, and
urged everyone to work harder for the great enterprise. His agents
scoured Europe for supplies: food, rope, timber, tar, canvas, nails, shoes.
No price was too high to pay for guns, gunpowder, and shot. Indeed,
for the right price, even certain English merchants were only too happy
to smuggle weapons.

The Armada finally assembled at Lisbon in the spring. Its total
strength was 130 vessels, including sixty-five galleons and great ships,

big merchantmen outfitted as warships. In addition, there were four galleasses, a cross between the galley and the galleon. Heavier than a galley, but lighter than a galleon, the galleasse was powered by oars and sails, and carried broadside guns on a deck built above the rowing benches. The rest of the Armada consisted of hospital ships, light scouting craft, and supply vessels. There were no galleys; these were too flimsy for the rough Atlantic.

In round numbers, the fleet was manned by 30,000 men: 8,000 sailors, 19,000 soldiers, and 3,000 "others." Spaniards were in the majority; the second largest group were Portuguese, followed by men from Philip's Italian possessions, Germans, Frenchmen, Flemings, and English traitors who would help govern their conquered country; hundreds of Negroes slaved aboard the galleasses. A hospital staff of sixty-two doctors and orderlies was to care for the men's bodies and 180 priests were to look after their souls. There were also 120 gentlemen adventurers and their 456 servants; no fashionable young man would go to war with fewer than three servants; one, the prince of Ascoli, brought thirty-nine servants. The gentlemen carried bags of gold coins sewn into their clothes and wore heavy gold chains around their necks; the links could be twisted off whenever they had to pay for something.

Popular songs and poems tell much about Spanish morale. It was high, as we learn from this jingle:

> *My brother Don John*
> *To England is gone,*
> *To kill the Drake*
> *And the Queen to take,*
> *And the heretics all to destroy.*[1]

Armada men often had a blood-red cross embroi-dered on their doublets to show they were going on a holy crusade. They felt that victory was certain, and would be easy, because they fought for God. An official proclamation, read by officers to their men, said: "We go on a task which offers no great difficulty, because God, in whose sacred cause we go, will lead us. With such a Captain we need have no fear."[2]

Religion, however, was mixed with worldlier motives. Time and again, soldiers' letters tell that their greatest fear was not of death, but that the English would surrender to save their country from pillage. Like the conquistadors, the Armada's men were going on a looting expedition. Their goal was not a town or a treasure ship, as with Drake, but an entire nation, as with Cortés and Pizarro. They meant to settle in the conquered country and live off its people.

ALEXANDER FARNESE, DUKE OF PARMA, WAS SPAIN'S LEADING GENERAL. ALTHOUGH HE COMMANDED THE INVASION TROOPS DESTINED FOR ENGLAND, HE BELIEVED THE ARMADA WAS DOOMED TO FAIL.

Had they known the truth, they would not have been so confident or greedy. Far from being the "Invincible Armada"—a sarcastic term invented after the Armada's failure—the expedition's weaknesses all but doomed it to failure. These weaknesses were three in number: its attack plan, its top command, and its ships.

King Philip had drawn up the plan in the quiet of the Escorial. Though he had never fought a battle, His Majesty thought he knew all there was to know about making war. His plan called for the Armada to sail up the English Channel, anchor at the mouth of the Thames River, and wait for the army of the Netherlands. That army was led by Alexander Farnese, duke of Parma, a military genius who had won important victories against the Dutch. Parma was to leave his bases at Dunkirk and Nieuport, join up with the Armada, and seize London. The Armada must not fight except in self-defense or to clear enemy vessels from its path. Its task was to guard the troopships, keeping the English fleet away from the landing sites.

It was a lovely plan—on paper. The problem lay in uniting a sea force and a land force. Timing is everything in such an operation. Each force must be in the right place at the right time, and there is little room for error. A land force putting to sea without a fleet's protection is an easy target for enemy cruisers prowling offshore. Nor can a fleet stay in one place very long without inviting attack or being scattered by storms.

Parma's fleet had hundreds of flat-bottomed canal barges, unarmed and without masts or sails. Left to themselves in the channel, they would be destroyed by the rebel Dutch Sea Beggars, who had a hundred and thirty flyboats, light gunboats able to sail in shallow waters. Parma, therefore, needed the navy to clear the way for his invasion craft. Unfortunately, the navy's ships were too big for inshore work. The Flemish coast was studded with submerged sandbanks, and they would run aground if they ventured close to shore. Thus, the two halves of the Enterprise of England could not be brought together.

His Majesty knew the facts, but misled his commanders. He told the navy that Parma had warships of his own and could easily get out of port. He told Parma that the navy would see to it that the army crossed without a fight. Worse, neither service understood what the other was supposed to be doing. Philip never asked the commanders to meet to discuss or criticize his plan. His Majesty never explained why he kept them in the dark. Perhaps he feared they would lose faith in the plan. Or, perhaps, he believed that since he was fighting a holy war, surely God would guarantee its success.

This was the way things stood when Santa Cruz died on February 9, 1588. Philip replaced him with Don Alonso Pérez de Guzmán el Bueno, duke of Medina Sidonia. At thirty-eight, Medina Sidonia, a quiet, melancholy person, was the nation's wealthiest nobleman, with 25,000 people living in scores of villages on his estates. He was also a brave bullfighter and a loyal Spaniard. In a country where rank counted

DON ALONZO PÉREZ DE GUZMÁN, DUKE OF MEDINA SIDONIA, TOOK OVER COMMAND OF THE ARMADA AFTER THE DEATH OF SANTA CRUZ. A MAN WHO EASILY BECAME SEASICK, HE KNEW HE WAS NOT QUALIFIED TO LEAD A FLEET INTO BATTLE.

for so much, he seemed the ideal commander. No one, even the most high-born, could resent serving under him.

The trouble was that Medina Sidonia did not want the job. He was an intelligent man and knew he was not qualified to lead the Armada, nor indeed any fighting force. He was horrified upon learning that Philip had "fixed his eye" upon him. He wrote a long letter to the king's secretary, explaining why he could not—*must not*—serve. It said in part:

> I humbly thank His Majesty for having thought of me for so great a
> task, and I wish I possessed the talents and strength necessary for it. But,
> Sir, I have no health for the sea, for I know by the small experience that
> I have had afloat that *I soon become seasick*. . . . The force is so great, and
> the undertaking so important, that it would not be right for a person like

myself, possessing no experience of seafaring or of war, to take charge of it. . . . *I possess neither aptitude, ability, health or fortune.* . . . For me to take charge of the Armada afresh, without the slightest knowledge of it. . . . would be simply groping in the dark. . . . So, Sir, you will see that my reasons for declining are so strong and convincing in His Majesty's own interests, that I cannot attempt a task of which I have no doubt I should give a bad account . . . for I do not understand it, know nothing about it, have no health for the sea, and no money to spend upon it.[3]

If the plea of poverty was silly, the rest was true. It must have hurt him to say so, for Medina Sidonia always put the interests of his country ahead of personal ambition. Philip, however, brushed his objections aside. "Do not bother us with fears about the success of the Armada," His Majesty wrote. "In such a cause God will assure a good outcome."[4] And so the seasick duke became Captain General of the Ocean Sea. He did the best he could, but he was no Santa Cruz—or Francis Drake. That was not his fault, but the king's for choosing him over some fine, if less well-born, naval commanders.

Finally, there was the Armada itself. Its backbone was the galleon, the basic warship of the sixteenth century. A vessel of between 250 and 1,100 tons, the galleon was about 150 feet long, 40 feet wide, and rose 35 feet from the waterline to the main deck. Built to fight, its hull was four to five feet thick, with a three-story wooden tower, or castle, rising above the bow and stern. These massive structures made the galleon top-heavy, slowing it down and causing it to roll in heavy seas. But that was not a serious problem, given Spanish battle tactics.

The tactics were a carryover from the Middle Ages, when ships were used as floating islands protected by the castle. The idea was to grapple with an enemy vessel, board it, and capture it with swords and pikes. A ship's deck was the true battlefield, a sea fight simply a land battle afloat.

Castles were both for attack and defense. During an attack the soldiers crowded in them poured arrows into the low "waist"—the middle part—of the enemy ship. If the enemy came aboard, they caught him in a crossfire in the waist of their own vessel. A Spanish naval captain, like an English sailing master, was responsible only for navigating the ship. In everything else, army officers told him what to do and when to do it. Common soldiers treated sailors as their servants; sailors carried the soldiers into action, but it was the soldiers who won the glorious victories. Richard Hawkins was right when he said Spanish sailors "are but the slaves of the rest, to moil and toil day and night."[5]

Even after ships started carrying guns in the 1400s, the Spanish stuck to the old ways. Galleons had from twenty-five to fifty heavy cannons on two gun decks. These were used not to sink the enemy, but to slow him down. Gunners fired on the upward roll, as their

A GALLEON IN ACTION. SPANISH GALLEONS, LIKE THE ONE SHOWN HERE, CARRIED SHORT-RANGE GUNS TO DISABLE ENEMY SHIPS AND MASSES OF SOLDIERS TO BOARD THEM. ENGLISH GALLEONS, HOWEVER, CARRIED MANY LONG-RANGE GUNS TO PREVENT BOARDING AND TO POUND ENEMY VESSELS TO BITS FROM A SAFE DISTANCE.

ship climbed a wave. The added height made it easier to bring down the enemy's masts, cut his rigging, and tear his sails. As he wallowed in the water, unable to make way, the attacker swept alongside for boarding. Now the battle really began. Musketeers had replaced archers in the castles, which now also bristled with small, quick-loading "murdering pieces." Each murdering piece fired bunches of musket balls, rusty nails, or scrap iron. Turned against boarding parties, or defenders, they had the effect of many huge shotguns going off at once.

These tactics had always worked against Spain's enemies. The English, however, played by different rules.

A NAVAL DESIGNER'S PLAN FOR AN ENGLISH GALLEON. NOTICE THAT IT IS BUILT LOW AND STREAMLINED, LIKE A FISH. THIS MADE IT FASTER AND EASIER TO HANDLE THAN THE SPANISH GALLEON.

*E*ngland's struggle has been likened to the fight between David and Goliath. A small fleet of tiny English Davids is supposed to have defeated a mass of hulking Spanish Goliaths. Not so. The Spanish ships looked bigger because of their high castles, but in fact, the English outclassed the enemy in every way. Not only did they have more ships, but they were larger, faster, and better armed than anything

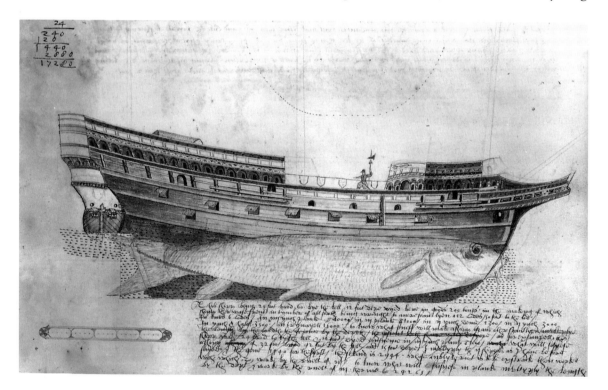

under the red and gold flag of Spain. In 1588, the English fleet had between 140 and 160 ships. The majority were divided into two battle squadrons, with the rest held in reserve as reinforcements. Thirty-six ships guarded the Straits of Dover at the channel's northern entrance and ninety were based at Plymouth. Most fighting ships were armed merchantmen, as with the enemy. Others were pinnaces and other small fry used in scouting and carrying messages. Twenty-seven were Queen's ships—the finest galleons afloat.

Drake and Hawkins had studied the problems of sea warfare from every angle. Their conclusion had been that England needed a new kind of ship for a new style of fighting. That ship must be a weapon for sailors rather than a floating battlefield for soldiers. A ship's captain must be in total command, as Drake had made clear when he beheaded Thomas Doughty. By 1588, his idea had become law aboard English warships.

After San Juan de Ulua, Hawkins settled into life ashore. He ran his shipping business and became Plymouth's leading citizen. In 1577, Her Majesty named him treasurer of the navy, a job once held by his father-in-law. The position had less to do with managing money than repairing existing ships and building new ones in the royal dockyards.

The appointment was the chance Hawkins needed. As galleons came in for repairs, he turned them into "race-built" ships. The word "race" comes from "raze," as in razing, or tearing down. Hawkins razed the ships' forecastles and lowered their sterncastles by at least 50 percent. New ships were built lower, longer, and narrower than the traditional galleon. The result was a streamlined vessel that was easier to handle and could sail rings around anything of equal size.

Despite changes over the next two centuries, Hawkins's basic design was used throughout the Age of Fighting Sail. The names of his ships had a modern ring to them: *Revenge* (500 tons), *Dreadnought* (400 tons), *Ark Royal* (800 tons), *Victory* (800 tons), *Elizabeth Jonas* (900 tons). The men who sailed aboard the USS *Constitution* ("Old Ironsides") would have felt at home on any of these beauties. The names of Spanish ships, in contrast, were straight out of the Middle Ages: *Nuestra Señora de la Rosa (Our Lady of the Rose), San Martín (St. Martin), Nuestra Señora del Rosario (Our Lady of the Rosary),* and *San Juan Bautista (St. John the Baptist).*

Spanish ships were man-carriers; Hawkins's were gun-carriers. Built as floating gun platforms, they had but one purpose: kill enemy ships, not enemy soldiers. Under no circumstances would the English try to board; that would be playing to the enemy's strength. They wanted an all-gun battle. They would fire on the downward roll, when the enemy was rising on one wave and they were sliding down another. The idea was to shatter the hull below the waterline, sending the ship to the bottom.

The opposing navies relied upon different types of guns. Spanish vessels mounted cannons and demicannons, short-barreled weapons (eight to ten feet long) that fired heavy balls short distances. Firing point-blank—the range at which a ball would hit its target if the gun barrel was horizontal—these could throw a 50-or 30-pound ball 500 yards, more or less. That is not very far, but far enough to cripple an enemy for boarding. The English, however, went in for culverins and demiculverins. The barrels of these weapons were 14 feet long, which meant they could only throw a 17- or 9-pound ball but it could travel about 700 yards. (A gun able to fire a heavy ball a great distance would have had to be 20 feet long, too big for the tight space of a galleon's gun deck.) English vessels, therefore, could not hit the enemy as hard as he could hit them. But they could hit him from farther away, without being hit in return and without fear of being boarded. They could also hit him more often, because a smaller cannon is easier to reload than a larger one.

The English made no secret of their ships and tactics. At Cadiz, the enemy had seen both in action. Spanish commanders, who knew the score, were unhappy. Fearing the worst, but hoping for the best, Juan Martínez de Recalde, one of Philip's most experienced admirals, put his trust in God alone. A church official asked him if he expected to defeat the English fleet in the Channel.

"Of course," de Recalde replied.

"How can you be sure?"

"It's very simple. It is well known that we fight in God's cause. So when we meet the English, God will surely arrange matters so that we can grapple and board them, either by sending some strange freak of weather or, more likely, just by depriving the English of their wits. If we can come to close quarters, Spanish valor and Spanish steel (and the great masses of soldiers we shall have on board) will make our victory certain. But unless God helps us by a miracle, the English, who have faster and handier ships than ours, and many more long-range guns . . . will never close with us at all, but stand aloof and knock us to pieces with their culverins, without our being able to do them serious hurt. So we are sailing to England in the confident hope of a miracle."[6]

The admiral may have believed that a miracle would happen—or was just making a clever joke at his king's expense.

Enemy ships and guns were not the Spaniards' only worry. The English leaders were top-notch. Drake, the nation's most famous seaman, seemed the natural choice to head the fleet. Yet no one, including Drake himself, expected him to get the post. Sea captains were proud, independent folks. Even though they called him "Sir," men like Hawkins and Frobisher resented having to take orders from one they considered an equal. The fiery Frobisher was so jealous that he insulted Drake behind his back, even spoke of challenging him to a duel.

Queen Elizabeth, like King Philip, needed someone of the highest social rank to command the fleet. She chose her cousin, Charles, Lord Howard of Effingham. Like his father and two uncles before him, Howard was lord high admiral of England, the navy's commander-in-chief. He had never fought a battle, but that did not matter; his true abilities lay in helping others work together and in knowing his own limitations. Unlike the Spanish king, he had sense enough to trust those who knew more than he and to take their advice.

LORD HOWARD OF EFINGHAM LED THE ENGLISH FLEET AGAINST THE SPANISH ARMADA. ALTHOUGH NOT AS ACCOMPLISHED A SEAMAN AS FRANCIS DRAKE, HE WAS A GREAT NOBLEMAN WHO COMMANDED HIS CAPTAIN'S RESPECT.

Drake was his chief adviser, or lieutenant to the lord high admiral, the fleet's acting battle commander. Howard relied on the preacher's son to make the key decisions, which he then supported. Sir Francis was proud to serve under such a great nobleman. Still, Howard's name meant little to the enemy. When Spaniards thought of English sea fighters, *El Draque* automatically came to mind. For them, the English fleet was always "Drake's fleet." If they were to win, he was the man to beat.

Meantime, the English home front prepared for the coming struggle. No effort was spared in arousing the nation's fighting spirit. The press encouraged people to resist to the last drop of their blood. Fear was a major tool in this effort. Pamphlets told of Armada ships filled with torture instruments. One galleon was supposed to be carrying only hangman's ropes; all Englishmen between the ages of twelve and seventy were to be executed the moment they fell into Spanish hands. Another vessel was said to carry whips to be used on English women; most would then be raped by enemy troops, killed, and their babies suckled by three thousand Spanish wet nurses brought along just for this purpose. Children between the ages of seven and twelve were to be branded on the face to mark them as slaves.

These claims seemed believable at the time. King Philip certainly meant to bring in the Inquisition once England was conquered, and everyone knew what *that* meant. Spanish atrocities in the Low Countries and the New World had been publicized for generations. After defeating the Aztecs, for example, Cortés marched lines of chained slaves in front of bonfires. As each person's turn came, a blacksmith drew a branding iron from the fire and burned the letter G for *guerra*, "war," into their lips and cheeks. An English translation of Bartholomé de las Casas's *Devastation of the Indies* had been printed in 1583 and became a bestseller. English people easily imagined themselves in the Indians' places.

The government took no chances with "security risks." Though the majority of Catholics were loyal, officials feared that several hundred diehards might join the invader. These were arrested and put where they could do no harm. The most dangerous wound up in the Tower of London, others in local jails. Foreigners were also viewed with suspicion; but instead of being arrested, they were kept under close watch. Still, the English distrusted them, and let them know it by coarse insults. Said an Italian living in London: "It is easier to find flocks of white crows than one Englishman . . . who loves a foreigner."[7]

The nation prepared to fight back by any and all means. To warn of the enemy's approach, beacons were set up along the coast and deep inland. If the Spanish came at night, iron baskets filled with pitch would be lit on hilltops and in church steeples. By day, damp hay would produce columns of smoke visible for miles in every direction. The sea was patrolled around the clock by fast ships disguised as harmless traders. Some vessels scouted off the Spanish coast, even prowled outside Spanish harbors. At the first sight of the Armada, they were to alert the fleet at Plymouth.

Plans called for meeting the invader at the water's edge. The most likely landing sites were protected by lines of trenches for musketeers and stakes planted on the beach. Caltrops, two iron spikes joined so that one would always point upward, were scattered along beaches to halt advancing cavalry.

If the Spaniards managed to break through the shore defenses, they faced bitter opposition. Because they "are fighting for country, faith, and children," an Italian diplomat who knew the English well predicted, the battle would be bloodier than any within memory; even the Dutch revolt would pale in comparison. "For the English never yield; and although they be put to flight and broken, they ever return, athirst for revenge, to renew the attack, so long as they have a breath of life."[8]

England had no standing army. Nevertheless, Her Majesty could count upon the "trained bands," thousands of armed volunteers. As war fever swept the nation, old-timers, rickety with age, promised to strike a blow for Good Queen Bess. In remote villages, boys drilled with homemade swords and pikes.

By late July, fifty thousand infantry and ten thousand cavalry had joined the colors. Hundreds of thousands of others stood ready for guerrilla warfare. Once the battle moved inland, they were to turn the countryside into a desert. They would burn crops, destroy bridges, and move cattle to keep them out of Spanish hands. Orders called for them to harass the invader day and night, striking when least expected and giving him no rest.

Experienced soldiers insisted the volunteers were no match for professionals, and those the finest in Europe. Men like Sir John ("Black

SOUTH SEA CASTLE, ONE OF ENGLAND'S COASTAL DEFENSES AT THE TIME
OF THE SPANISH ARMADA. FORTIFICATIONS SUCH AS THIS WERE DESIGNED
NOT TO DEFEAT AN INVASION FORCE, BUT TO SLOW IT UP LONG ENOUGH
FOR ENGLISH LAND FORCES TO PREPARE TO MEET THE ENEMY.

Jack") Norreys, a tough general who had served with the Dutch, said he "trembled" for his country. So did Lord Howard. He prayed for "God [to] send us the happiness to meet the Spaniards" before the men on land met them.[9] Only England's sailors could save the nation.

*T*he Armada sailed on May 30, 1588, with the blessings of the church. Things went wrong from the outset. It had hardly cleared the coast, when a storm struck. Sailors, who had seen worse, were not fazed. For the soldiers, however, it was something else.

Because they were landlubbers for the most part, going to sea was a terrifying experience for a soldier. Life on board had been all right in port, where you could go ashore to stretch your legs, and where the ships stood still and the hatches were kept open to let in air. At sea, the hatches were shut and the air became foul. Soldiers slept on the bare decks, packed shoulder to shoulder like slaves, only without being chained.

The storm made a bad situation unbearable. Soldiers turned green from seasickness and swore it was the end of the world; Medina Sidonia was probably sicker than most, but he had the luxury of a bed in a large private cabin. Soldiers, too ill to go topside, vomited into buckets; when these filled to overflowing, or were not within easy reach, they used any corner they could find. The decks stank like open sewers.

By burning all those barrel staves the year before, Drake was now killing the troops without firing a shot. Spanish coopers had been forced to use improperly seasoned wood. Food and water, kept in the holds for weeks, spoiled. Especially the water. Not only was water scarce, it was often green and slimy. Men drank it anyway, because it seemed better than nothing. But it was like swallowing poison. Each day, hundreds came down with diarrhea, and dozens died.

On June 19, the Armada limped into Corunna on Spain's northern coast. In nearly three weeks, it had covered little more than three hundred miles! Medina Sidonia ordered fresh water and provisions, and tried to replace the men he had lost. It wasn't easy. Word of the voyage thus far had swept through the coastal villages. Sailors went into hiding rather than join the Armada, forcing the duke to use farmers taken at gunpoint from their fields. Armed guards were posted to prevent desertions.

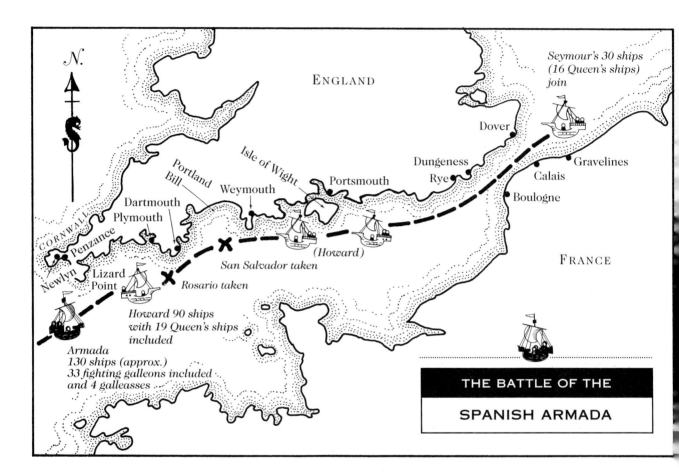

THE BATTLE OF THE

SPANISH ARMADA

Medina Sidonia was doing his duty, but deep down he had lost hope. The Armada had faced its first test—and failed miserably. He was so upset that he wrote the king, suggesting the voyage be postponed a year. He even urged Philip to avoid war "by making some honorable terms with the enemy." That was excellent advice, for Queen Elizabeth would have jumped at the chance to avoid bloodshed. Unfortunately, the king had his heart set on war. "I have dedicated this enterprise to God," he replied impatiently. "Get on, then, and do your part."[10]

The Armada left Corunna on July 22. This time it had a favorable wind and made good headway. At four o'clock in the afternoon of Friday, July 29, one of the duke's naval aides pointed out a distant piece of land. Lizard Point, England.

That night, off "the Lizard," the *San Martín*, Medina Sidonia's flagship, fired a salute. Instantly a sacred banner unfurled at the top of her mainmast. Blessed by the church, it bore Spain's coat of arms bordered on one side by the image of Christ crucified, on the other by the Virgin Mary. Beneath was a scroll with the Latin motto, *Exurge domine et vindicta causam tuam,* "Arise, O Lord, and vindicate Thy cause." Three more guns were fired, the signal for everyone to go down on his knees in prayer.

The outline of the coast was visible even in the dark. As the Armada advanced, beacons flared on the shore behind it, alongside it, and far ahead of it. The war flames raced inland, and church bells clanged. All over England men rolled out of bed, threw on their clothes, and grabbed their weapons. Soon town streets and country lanes were filled with men hurrying to their assembly points.

No one slept in Plymouth. Earlier in the day, on the pinnace *Golden Hind,* Captain Thomas Fleming had sighted the Armada off the Lizard. Legend has it that Drake and his captains were playing a game of bowls on the hoe, the open ground between the town and the sea, when the news came. The officers were excited, but Drake is supposed to have said, "Play out the game; there is time enough for that and to beat the Spanish after." This seems like an odd thing to say, with the enemy barely fifty miles away. Yet he probably did say something very close to it.

There *was* enough time. High tide was rushing into the harbor, and the fleet could not go anywhere until it slackened in a few hours. Even so, Drake certainly ordered the ships to be made ready in a hurry. Off-duty crewmen had to be rounded up and the remaining supplies taken aboard.

Meantime, Medina Sidonia had called a council of war aboard *San Martín.* Vice-Admiral Juan Martínez de Recalde and other navy men saw a golden opportunity. The tide, they knew, would trap the English fleet at Plymouth. By sending their fastest galleons ahead, they could enter the harbor on the flood. The enemy, caught with his anchors down, would be helpless. Using their heavy short-range guns, the Spaniards could easily disable English vessels and take them by boarding. The duke, however, refused to act. King Philip's orders were clear: he must only fight in self-defense. Thus, the "crowned slave" in the Escorial forced his commander to throw away Spain's best, and only, hope of victory.

DRAKE'S GAME OF BOWLS AS IMAGINED BY AN ARTIST. THE ENGLISH CAPTAINS HAD PLENTY OF TIME ON THEIR HANDS WHILE THEIR SHIPS WERE BEING LOADED AND BEFORE THE TIDE TURNED, ENABLING THEM TO SAIL FROM PLYMOUTH HARBOR.

The English made their move in the early morning hours of July 30. With the tide slackening, the fleet began to warp anchors. One end of a cable was attached to each ship, the other end to a small anchor, or kedge, which was lowered into a longboat. The anchor was then rowed ahead about a hundred yards and dropped overboard. The ship's crew then gave a heave-ho on the cable, pulling their vessel forward; aboard *Ark Royal*, the flagship, Lord Howard grabbed a rope and pulled along with his men. The anchor was hauled up and the process repeated until every vessel cleared Plymouth harbor.

Throughout the day, the fleets went about their business without making contact. At daybreak, Sunday, July 31, they saw each other for the first time. The Spaniards were astonished. After the Spanish ships had reached the channel, the English had done some fancy sailing and had slipped behind the Armada, gaining a critical advantage. Remember, sailing ships depend upon the wind. In a sea fight, ships might come at each other from a windward (upwind) or a leeward (downwind) position. A vessel in the windward position has the "weather gauge," that is, the wind is at its back, filling its sails. It can attack whenever it wishes, and do so faster. Because the leeward vessel must turn into the wind and tack (zigzag) from side to side, it is slower and harder to handle. Until the wind shifts or dies, ships holding the weather gauge can fight or break off action as they please.

The Armada had lost the wind. For the next eight days, it blew from the southwest, up the channel. This allowed the English to pounce on any outlying vessels, while Spanish rescuers had to beat against the wind. Only the galleasses could get to the rear quickly enough to be a serious threat.

The Armada was awesome, at once beautiful and menacing. Each ship was a work of art with a brilliantly painted hull, gilt carvings at bow and stern, and a giant red cross painted on the foresails. The fleet was enormous; so large, in fact, that eyewitnesses said "the ocean groaned under its weight." Its formation, shaped roughly like a half-moon, was

THE SPANISH ARMADA OFF PLYMOUTH, WITH THE ENGLISH FLEET GETTING INTO POSITION TO ATTACK FROM THE REAR.

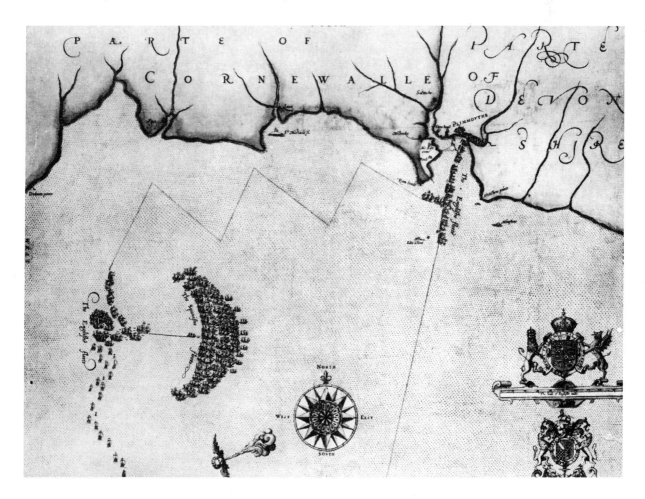

thick at the center, with two long "wings" tapering backward. To keep together, it moved at barely two miles an hour, the speed of the slowest vessels. Three galleasses led the way, followed by *San Martín* and the "main battle," twenty galleons from Spain and Portugal. A mass of troopships and supply ships came next. Trailing behind them, forming the wings, was the rear guard, four squadrons of armed merchantmen and a galleasse on the extreme right.

Battle stations! Drummers and trumpeters in both fleets sounded the urgent call. Before they'd finished, the sound of bare feet slapping on wood was coming from every corner of every ship. Each man knew where he belonged and what he had to do. Topmen scrambled aloft up rope ladders to take in or let out sail on command. Musketeers manned the fighting tops, platforms set high on the masts. Deckhands hung nets under the masts to catch falling debris and around the ship's waist to entangle boarders. Their most important task, however, was fire control. Each side had its own fire-making devices, usually thrown by hand at close range. The Spaniards favored "firepots," clay jars filled with naphtha, a colorless liquid made from oil. The English preferred "fire wings," grenades studded with barbed nails that stuck in wood, and flaming arrows. To contain the damage, sailors wrapped masts and other flammable equipment in wet burlap, and hoisted aloft buckets of water to be poured over the sails.

Below decks was a scene of frenzied activity. Carpenters prepared to close holes with layers of tarred canvas; divers plugged holes below the waterline with sheets of lead. The surgeon laid out his saws and knives, needles and drills, on a table set on the ballast. The same instruments were used on one patient after another, washed only after the day's work, as were the surgeon's hands. Operating tables were bare wooden planks set between barrels. Not all wounded, however, would see the surgeon. Badly wounded men were flung overboard to put them out of their misery; the dead went overboard so as not to clutter the narrow decks.

The gun decks were busiest. Officers barked orders. Ammunition carriers brought gunpowder and shot from the magazine. Some gunners stacked shot in piles beside their weapons, while others filled buckets with vinegar to clean out the barrel each time it was fired. After loading their weapons, they opened the ports, hinged doors that lifted upward, and rolled the guns into firing position. Each gun had a crew of eight to ten men, depending on its size.

Naval guns fired different types of shot for different purposes. *Solid shot*, the most common, was an iron ball used to punch holes in an enemy's hull. *Bar shot*, resembling weightlifters' barbells, tumbled as it flew, as did *chain shot*, two cannon balls joined by a chain. Both could smash masts and spars, or smash a man to a bloody pulp. *Carcasses* were hollow balls filled with materials for starting fires from a distance. *Langerill shot* were canisters filled with jagged pieces of iron that burst open, showering their contents over a wide area.

The battle began when a lone English pinnace broke away from the main body of the fleet. She belonged to Lord Howard and was called *Disdain*, a fitting name for her mission today. Racing ahead, she closed with one of the great ships of the Armada's rear guard. Then she hove to, fired her tiny popgun, and sped away before the enemy could reply. *Disdain* had delivered England's challenge to Spain, and by doing so made history. For that single shot opened the first fleet-to-fleet gun battle of all time.

The English galleons sped downwind in line-ahead formation. Their target was not the Armada's thick center, but the tips of its exposed wings. Lord Howard in the *Ark Royal* charged the right wing; Drake, in the *Revenge*, led the assault on the left wing, joined by Hawkins in the *Victory* and Frobisher in the *Triumph*. Seeing his ships in trouble, Medina Sidonia turned back into the wind to help. One by one, other galleons joined in the rescue effort.

As the English closed the distance, the leader of each line fired a broadside from his starboard guns and kept going to allow the ship behind to fire, then the next, and so on down the line. Tongues of orange flame lashed out from the side of each vessel, followed by the whoosh and whine of cannon balls speeding through the air. Meantime, the leader wheeled around to fire another broadside from his port guns, giving the first crews time to reload.

Handling guns was work for experts. Each step in their operation had to be done correctly, otherwise they misfired or, worse, exploded.

Load. Gunpowder held in a long wooden ladle was poured down the cannon's muzzle, followed by a wad of shredded rope which was packed tightly with a rammer, a large wooden knob at the end of a pole. You had to use just the right amount of gunpowder; too little would make a bright flash and nothing more, too much could make the gun explode. Next, a ball was rolled down the muzzle and rammed

A SIXTEENTH-CENTURY NAVAL GUN. THE INSTRUMENTS ON THE DECK, BEHIND THE GUNNER, WERE USED TO SWAB THE BARREL AFTER EACH SHOT, INSERT A FRESH GUN- POWDER CHARGE, AND RAM A CANNON BALL DOWN THE MUZZLE.

tight with another rope wad on top. Lastly, fine-grained gunpowder was poured into the touchhole at the rear of the weapon.

Aim. Unlike modern artillery, sixteenth-century guns had no aiming devices. For turning right and left, the entire gun mount, a four-wheeled wooden carriage, had to be swung into position by hand. The barrel was raised or lowered by inserting or removing wooden wedges called quoins, or coins.

Fire. The gun captain held a "match," a slow-burning rope attached to a forked stick called a linstock; the stick was often carved to resemble a snake or crocodile. When he put the match to the touchhole, there was a loud *huff,* followed by a jet of flame that scorched the timbers overhead. The gunpowder in the barrel ignited, turning the gun into a roaring, kicking, flame-spitting monster. The explosion set off shock waves that could collapse the eardrums of anyone who had not tied a kerchief around his ears. And the gun recoiled so quickly that anyone not fast enough might have both legs crushed.

Sponge and reload. After each shot, soot and smoldering bits of rope stuck to the inside of the barrel and had to be cleaned out with a "sponge," a mop made of sheepskin wool dipped in vinegar; awful things happened when fresh gunpowder was ladled into a poorly cleaned barrel.

In later centuries, a well-trained gun crew could load, fire, sponge, and reload within two minutes. That was after experience gained in countless sea fights; there had never been an all-gun fleet action before 1588. Experts believe the English needed five minutes to load and fire a culverin; each gun fired twelve times an hour. The Spaniards took fifteen minutes to load and fire their heavy cannons. Some Spanish guns were so poorly made that they had to cool for an hour before being reloaded. Even then, several exploded, killing their crews.

A galleon firing a broadside burned about four hundred pounds of gunpowder each time. Smoke built up faster than it could escape through the gun ports. Men saw each other as ghostly shadows moving through thick fog. They coughed and wheezed and gasped for air. Their eyes stung and tears ran down their cheeks. Particles of soot clung to their bodies, turning them black as coal. Sweat came from every pore, causing unquenchable thirst.

At one o'clock in the afternoon, Lord Howard raised a signal flag to break off the battle. Commanders in both fleets were dissatisfied with the results. They had slugged it out for nearly eight hours. Though scores of men had been killed, mostly soldiers on the Spaniards' upper decks, no ships were seriously damaged, let alone sunk. All of which proves that war planning is not an exact science. One can plan carefully and still overlook important details.

Each side had a different style of fighting, and neither worked. The Spaniards wanted to fight at close quarters and board, but the English never let them near enough. As Medina Sidonia wrote in his log: "Their ships are so fast and so nimble they can do anything they like with them."[11] The English wanted to pound from a safe distance, but their light culverin balls could not crack the enemy's hulls unless they came closer, exposing themselves to the Spaniards' heavy guns. That, Howard explained, was suicide: "We durst not adventure to put in among them, their fleet being so strong."[12] Day One had been a standoff. There could be no victory until one side ran out of ammunition or something made the Armada break formation.

The worst Spanish losses came after the battle. One of their finest galleons, the one thousand-ton *Nuestra Señora del Rosario*, slammed into another vessel while turning. Down went her foremast, which struck the mainmast, weakening it and causing it to fall in a gust of wind. Medina Sidonia was coming to its assistance when the *San Salvador*, a galleon loaded with spare ammunition and carrying most of the

Armada's money, blew up nearby. The explosion may have been accidental, or, as some said, the revenge of a German gunner who had been beaten by an army captain. Whatever the cause, *San Salvador*'s stern was smashed and her sterncastle a heap of rubble. Two hundred men were killed outright or drowned when they jumped overboard. Rescuers found the decks slippery with blood; chunks of flesh lay around, and a head rolled from side to side across the deck. A rising wind made the wrecks unmanageable, and they were abandoned. The Armada continued up-channel, past Plymouth.

That night, Drake was leading the English fleet in the *Revenge* with only a lantern showing in her stern. Suddenly the lantern went out. Without their leader, and not daring to light their own lanterns, a number of ships strayed off course. Drake later said he had sighted strange vessels and, fearing the Spaniards were about to regain the weather gauge, went after them. The lantern, he said, had been put out so as not to alert the enemy. Although the strangers turned out to be German cargo ships on a routine voyage, the effort was not without value, at least to Drake.

At daybreak, August 1, he found *Nuestra Señora del Rosario* adrift. Crossing the T, he called for her to surrender or fight, according to the rules of war. That was a serious threat, since the rules allowed mercy to be shown to an enemy who surrendered when asked, but once blood was spilled, it was legal and proper to massacre all prisoners. Don Pedro de Valdez, *Rosario*'s captain, struck his colors and surrendered; indeed, he thought it an honor to be taken by the famous *El Draque*. That lucky meeting brought Drake a large share of a valuable ship and the 52,000 gold ducats found in her strongboxes. The smoldering wreck of the *San Salvador* was towed into an English port later that morning. Her treasure had been removed by the Spaniards, but she still had hundreds of pounds of usable gunpowder aboard.

Battles were fought on August 2 and 3 off Portland Bill and on August 4 near the Isle of Wight. Again there was plenty of shooting and little damage. Both sides were running low on ammunition by then, but the English had the edge. Fighting close to home, they could resupply the fleet as quickly as ammunition could be found ashore. Nevertheless, there were constant shortages, forcing some gunners to fire bunches of ploughchains instead of cannon balls.

There was no fighting on August 5, and Lord Howard used the lull to divide his fleet into four squadrons headed by himself, Drake,

Hawkins, and Frobisher. Each would follow the same line-ahead tactics that had been used since the outset. For good measure, he knighted Hawkins and Frobisher for their services at the Isle of Wight.

On August 6, the Armada anchored off the French port of Calais. Medina Sidonia could not enter the harbor, because France was neutral and did not want a quarrel with England. Besides, seeking shelter there was like sailing into a bag and leaving the drawstring in enemy hands; the English would surely trap him if he went inside. Nor could he stay outside for very long, either, thanks to strong crosscurrents.

Medina Sidonia sent an urgent message to Parma. The duke said the navy needed the army's help at once. To continue up-channel, he must have the support of "forty or fifty" of Parma's warships, plus any ammunition he could spare. Parma's reply must have hit him like a ton of bricks. The army, he wrote, had only flat-bottomed barges; even if

THE SPANISH ARMADA PURSUED UP THE ENGLISH CHANNEL BY THE ENGLISH FLEET. AS THE CAMPAIGN CONTINUED, MORE AND MORE SHIPS JOINED THE ENGLISH FLEET UNTIL IT OUTNUMBERED THE ENEMY.

it had warships, the Sea Beggars would slaughter them the moment they left port. Medina Sidonia should do the best he could with what he had. And until he cleared away the Dutch, the army would stay put. Thus, the Spanish commanders learned the truth. They had trusted their king's word, and he had lied. Convinced that God was on Spain's side, His Majesty was counting on miracles.

Early in the evening of Sunday, August 7, Medina Sidonia called a meeting to discuss the situation. There were no easy answers, and every choice carried dreadful risks. Turning back would mean more battles with dwindling ammunition supplies. A landing on the English coast with only the Armada's troops could easily end in disaster. Should the Armada try to find a safe port and await reinforcements? In the end, the English decided its next move.

Later that night, lookouts aboard the *San Martín* saw strange ships moving in from the north. The Dover patrol had arrived, bringing English fighting strength to over a hundred and forty vessels. For the first time, the Spaniards were outnumbered.

Medina Sidonia's captains knew what they would do were the situation reversed: use fire ships. Even thinking about fire ships sent chills down their spines. True, they had used them before, as at San Juan de Ulua and Cadiz. In 1585, however, they had met the "devil ships of Antwerp." During Parma's siege of that city, the defenders had turned two ships into floating bombs. Filling each with three-and-a-half tons of gunpowder, they sent them against a Spanish position, killing a thousand soldiers and wounding Parma. The idea that the English might use such weapons terrified the Spaniards. "We rode there at anchor all night," wrote an officer aboard the *San Martín*, ". . . and we waited because there was nothing else we could do. We had a great presentment of evil from those fiendish people and their arts."[13]

The "fiends" *were* preparing fire ships, but not of the devil-ship variety. Drake contributed the two-hundred-ton *Thomas*; Hawkins and six other captains gave vessels of about equal size. Each was loaded with barrels of tar and bundles of wood soaked in pitch, with their guns set to go off when the flames reached them.

Shortly after midnight, Spanish lookouts noticed pinpoints of light drifting away from the English fleet. Eight fire ships, sailing line abreast, were coming at them! Each vessel was manned by two or three volunteers with orders to start the fires, steer as close to the Armada as possible, and escape in rowboats at the last moment.

The pinpoints of light grew larger, larger, as if hell was about to break loose. The vessels were outlined in fire against the night sky. Flames ran up their rigging and ignited their sails. Tar melted, and bubbled, and flared. Showers of sparks leaped upward. Guns went off with a terrific roar, hurling hot iron in all directions. A Spaniard described how dreadful the ships looked, "spurting fire and their ordnance shooting, which was a horror to see in the night."[14]

Medina Sidonia had posted pinnaces to push them aside, but the fire ships were too big and too hot to approach. Borne on the wind and the incoming tide, they slipped past the screen and kept going. The duke's orders were that if this happened, captains must tie their anchor cables to buoys, cut them and move out of the way, returning for them later. But the captains were tired and jumpy after all they had been through. Suddenly, pent-up fears gave way to panic. Amid shouts that "the devil ships are coming," they cut their anchor cables and made sail.

A SAILOR'S WORST NIGHTMARE! DURING THE ARMADA'S LAYOVER AT THE FRENCH PORT OF CALAIS, THE ENGLISH SET SEVERAL OLD SHIPS AFIRE AND SENT THEM TOWARD LAND ON THE EVENING TIDE. THIS ACTION DROVE THE SPANIARDS OUT OF THE HARBOR IN CONFUSION, MAKING THEM GOOD TARGETS FOR THE WAITING ENGLISH FLEET.

The discipline that had held the Armada together cracked during that mad scramble to put to sea. Ships slammed into one another, doing more damage than all the English guns thus far. The fire ships, however, soon drifted to shore and burned themselves out. "The enemy were lucky," a Spaniard recalled, "their trick turned out exactly as they had planned. With eight ships they put us to flight, a thing they had not dared to attempt with a hundred and thirty."[15]

Monday, August 8. Daybreak revealed a scene to gladden English hearts. There was no more half-moon. The Armada lay scattered from Calais to Gravelines ten miles to the northeast. But not for long, since Medina Sidonia was proving to be a better commander than anyone expected, including himself. Once the fire ships had drifted away, he hove-to and reanchored. At dawn, *San Martín* fired signal guns to rally the fleet. The call was heard, and already several galleons were taking positions around the flagship.

Four English squadrons, including the Dover patrol, swung into action. Lord Howard's squadron missed the opening of the battle. As he bore down, he saw a juicy target stranded at the harbor entrance. *San Lorenzo*, flagship of the galleasses, had lost her rudder in a collision during the night. Running aground on a sandbar near Calais Castle, she lay on her side, her guns tilted and useless. Since the water was too shallow for the galleons, Howard sent fifteen longboats filled with sailors to finish her off. After a brief fight, in which *San Lorenzo*'s captain, Don Hugo de Moncada, fell with a musket ball between the eyes, the crew surrendered. The governor of Calais was willing to allow the English to loot the prize, but claimed the vessel itself for his country. Several French gentlemen came aboard with the message, only to be robbed by the sailors. Outraged at such bad manners, the governor turned the castle's guns on the galleasse. The sailors went scurrying back to their own vessels.

Meantime, the battle raged. Named for Gravelines, the town closest to the main action, it was to be the decisive battle of the campaign.

Gravelines was a gigantic brawl in which the English soon gained the upper hand. The Spaniards were running out of cannon balls. Gradually their fire slackened and, in some ships, ceased altogether. The English could now come in close and even stand a mere few yards from the towering galleons. At last, after three battles, their culverins were hitting with devastating effect.

Proud Spaniards were reduced to shooting musket balls while the English used cannon balls. This kind of fighting spirit had made the Spanish armies the terror of Europe. Glorious it may have been, but it was useless.

The Spanish ships became slaughter pens. Solid shot pierced their hulls, showering the decks with jagged splinters and leaving them awash in blood. Ships, streams of blood flowing over their sides, left red wakes behind them in the sea. No one on either side left a record of how it felt to see such sights. The closest we get to a firsthand account is a letter from a soldier named Pedro Estrade to his brother. "This day," Pedro writes, "was slain [a fine nobleman], with a bullet that struck off his head and splashed with his brains the greatest friend that he had there, and 24 men that were with us trimming the foresail. . . . And, as I was

AN ARTIST'S VIEW OF THE BATTLE OF GRAVELINES, AUGUST 8, 1588. THIS WAS THE ENGLISH FLEET'S LAST, AND BLOODIEST, ENCOUNTER WITH THE SPANISH ARMADA.

below in the afternoon . . . there was a mariner that had his leg struck all in pieces and died presently."[16] Playwright Lope de Vega took it all in a stride. As cannon balls whizzed by, he sat in a crow's nest writing poetry "to exercise my pen."[17]

San Martín and her escorts took a terrific beating. The flagship was riddled with shot and would have sunk had it not been for her carpenters and divers. Nearby, *San Felipe*'s guns fell silent and seventeen ships swept in for the kill. Taking pity, an English officer promised good terms if she surrendered. A musketeer shot him dead. As the English pulled out of range, the Spaniards shouted across, "calling them Lutheran hens, and daring them to return to the fight."[18] The bombardment continued without mercy. *San Mateo* tried to help, only to be attacked by ten ships. One Englishman, wild with excitement, leaped aboard the *San Mateo* by himself. "Our men cut him to bits instantly," a Spaniard reported.[19]

The battle had begun at seven in the morning. By four o'clock in the afternoon, the Armada was in bad shape. Lord Howard, who had finally joined the battle, would have pressed the attack had it not been for a violent squall. Seeing it coming, the English turned into the wind and shortened sail to avoid running into each other. For fifteen minutes, the fleets were lashed by blinding rain. By the time the rain stopped, the Spaniards were out of range and re-forming. The Battle of Gravelines was over.

It had been a good day for the English. Four of the Armada's finest ships were gone. *San Lorenzo* never got off the sandbank; years later, the French broke her up for her timber. *San Felipe* and *San Mateo* were abandoned and taken by the Sea Beggars. Before it was set adrift, *San Felipe*'s crew was put aboard other ships. *San Mateo*'s crew was less fortunate. Overtaken by a swarm of flyboats, they refused to surrender and fought for two hours before being overwhelmed. Then the law of war took effect; except for a handful of officers worth ransom money, the crew was thrown overboard. A great ship, the *María Juan*, was the last victim. Leaking like a sieve, she sank with 257 men aboard.

Medina Sidonia reported six hundred dead and eight hundred wounded in the day's action, compared to not more than one hundred English dead in the entire campaign. The Spaniards had fired 123,790 cannon balls in four battles, without seriously damaging an English ship. A careful survey after the battle showed that no enemy shot had broken through an English hull. The reasons for this are easy to see. Not only had the English kept out of range, but the Spanish cannon balls were defective. Divers have recently salvaged cannon balls from the wrecks of Armada ships. Many were made of impure iron so brittle as to shatter upon impact. Finally, the majority of Spanish gunners were soldiers with no experience in firing from the deck of a moving ship. English gunners, on the other hand, were all seamen.

As night fell, Drake sat at a table in his cabin. He was exhausted, but still had one more duty to perform before turning in. Taking out pen and paper, he scribbled a note to Walsingham: "I hope to God the Prince of Parma and the Duke of Medina Sidonia shall not shake hands. . . . Your honor's most ready to be commanded, but now half sleeping, Fra. Drake."[20]

Tuesday, August 9. At daybreak, Spanish lookouts saw the enemy in position a mile away. Again drums and trumpets sounded battle stations. The crews tensed to receive the attack, but the English kept their distance. After a while, the Spaniards understood why: the enemy was waiting for nature to do his work. Gazing to leeward, they saw long streaks of yellowish foam between them and the shore. Slowly but surely, the wind was driving the Spanish ships toward the Banks of Zeeland, submerged sandbanks that stretched for miles along the coast north of Gravelines. If they ran aground, the waves would batter them to pieces. "It was the most awful day in the world," an officer recalled. "Everyone was in utter despair and stood waiting for death."[21]

Thousands of men knelt in prayer, begging God for a miracle. Then, at the last moment, the wind shifted, carrying the Armada into deep water. The Spaniards finally had a "miracle," although not the one their king expected. The English watched, and wondered, and pondered the mysterious ways of the Lord.

Driven past Parma's bases in the Low Countries, their ammunition nearly gone, the Spaniards had no choice but to set a course for home. And since the enemy controlled the channel, that meant a long voyage northwestward around the British Isles. Her Majesty's fleet followed them up the east coast of Scotland, not to fight but to make sure the Spaniards kept going. The British couldn't fight; for they, too, had little ammunition. On August 12, with the danger past, they turned back.

On shore, preparations were still underway to meet the expected invasion. Every day more volunteers arrived at the main camp at

Tilbury on the Thames, just east of London. On August 18, Queen Elizabeth came to review the troops and stiffen their morale. Everyone expected her to move through the ranks surrounded by a large body-guard. Instead, she had only a four-man escort. She came all in white, riding a white horse and wearing white velvet. After the review, she gave a speech worthy of a great ruler who knew her power came from the people:

> Let tyrants fear! I have always so behaved myself that, under God,
> I have placed my chiefest strength and safeguard in the loyal hearts
> and goodwill of my subjects; and therefore I am come amongst
> you. . . . I know I have the body of a weak and feeble woman, but
> I have the heart and stomach of a king, and a king of England,
> too, and think foul scorn that Parma and Spain, or any prince
> of Europe, should dare to invade the borders of my realm; to which,
> rather than any dishonor shall grow by me, I myself will take up arms,
> I myself will be your general, judge, and rewarder of every one of your
> virtues in the field. I know already . . . [that] you have deserved
> rewards . . . and we do assure you on the word of a prince,
> they shall be duly paid you.[22]

Elizabeth surely meant what she said, but war expenses had practically emptied the Royal Treasury. To save money, the ships' crews had to be discharged as soon as the danger passed. But that could not happen until they were paid off. Until the government raised more money, they must remain aboard their ships.

Conditions aboard ship were bad and getting worse. Sailors had not washed or changed their clothes in weeks. Food was scarce, and much of what they had was rotten. By late August, twin epidemics were racing through the fleet. Dirt brought typhus fever and bad food caused food poisoning—by far the worst killer.

The lord high admiral ordered the men ashore in an effort to save their lives, only to find that it was like leaping from the frying pan into the fire. Without money or a place to stay, men who had saved their country died in the streets of its coastal towns. Howard dug into his own pockets to pay off as many as he could, and even took some of the money Drake found in the *Rosario*. Had he done less, he confessed, "I should have wished myself out of this world."[23] Nevertheless, his efforts were too little and too late.

As treasurer of the navy, Hawkins drew up casualty figures for each vessel. His figures are incomplete, but what they show is bad enough. The original crew of the *Bear*, for example, died off and was replaced twice; of the 1,000 men who served in a six-week period, only 250, or 25 percent, survived. *Triumph* lost 350 men from a company of 500 and *Elizabeth Jonas* 250 out of 500. No figures are available for Drake's *Revenge*, but there is no reason to believe they were better. In all, the fleet lost between four and five thousand men to disease, at least forty for every one killed by enemy action. Hawkins was horrified. The treasurer's job, he wrote, was killing him—and he was glad. "My pain and misery in this service is infinite," he wrote. "God, I trust, will deliver me of it ere it be long, for there is no other hell!"[24]

*T*he Armada sailed up the Scottish coast, then swung westward into the North Atlantic. This was no place for wooden ships with serious battle damage. The Atlantic swell, waves rolling free for three thousand miles, battered them constantly. Unseasonal storms tossed them about, driving icy water over the decks and down into the holds. "There were chills so cold that they made it seem like Christmas time," a priest recalled.[25]

The fleet broke up in more ways than one. No longer able to keep formation, ships separated into small groups or went on alone, each at its own speed. Certain vessels literally fell apart. Hulls began to flex under the impact of the waves. Planks loosened and caulking worked its way out. This, in turn, made the trenails—the wooden pegs that held planks to the ship's frames—come loose. The only thing to do was for everyone to work the pumps day and night, strenuous work even for healthy men.

The men of the Armada were far from healthy. An estimated one in five lay sick or wounded. The rest were starving on a daily ration of a pint of water, half a pint of wine, and half a pound of moldy biscuit. Things became so bad that soldiers stole sailors' rations at gunpoint and men sold their clothes for a few drops of water. They soon fell behind in their work, water built up in the holds, and the ship finally broke apart. Three vessels sank in this way off northern Scotland.

Ireland was worse. The western coast of the Emerald Isle is as treacherous as it is beautiful. Rugged cliffs and submerged rocks, riptides and storms, are still a menace to traffic in these waters. The more so when, as with the Spaniards, there are no accurate charts or pilots to show the way.

Twenty-six ships were wrecked on the Irish coast. Entire crews died within a few terrifying minutes. They went down with their vessels, drowned because they could not swim or were dragged under by the gold chains around their necks. Three galleons sank between Sligo and Ballyshannon, a mere five-mile stretch of coast, leaving the beach strewn with piles of wreckage and over twelve hundred bodies. Many, no doubt, had been allowed to drown by the superstitious natives. In old Ireland, people believed that anyone caught in the sea belonged to Lir, the pagan sea god. Saving them was robbing Lir, so that the rescuer or a member of his family would have to take their place.

Those who managed to stumble ashore often had their skulls crushed by the Irish. Many wandered about until killed by soldiers or handed over to English death squads.

It would seem that the Irish should have welcomed fellow Catholics. There were such people, of course; they helped several hundred escape to Scotland. Others, however, were desperately poor. Armada survivors were human gold mines, in their eyes. It was easy to kill them, take their money, and strip the bodies of their fine clothes. Those who turned in Spaniards did so out of fear; the English automatically killed anyone who sheltered a fugitive, along with his family. Most Irish killers were on the English payroll, carrying out English orders. They were thugs like Melaghlin McCabb, who butchered eighty Spaniards with an axe.

The killings were justified—or so the English said. Sir William Fitzwilliam, the governor, had two thousand poorly trained soldiers to hold down a rebellious nation. He could not risk having thousands of Spaniards in Ireland, even as war prisoners. Their very presence, he feared, would ignite another rebellion. Once freed, the prisoners would be able to mount a serious threat not only to English rule in Ireland, but to England itself. Ireland is a natural stepping stone for an invader. In the north, it is twelve miles from Scotland; in the east, you can see Wales on a clear day. In such a situation, terror seemed the best policy. Fitzwilliam's order was brief and brutal: "Apprehend and execute all Spaniards."[26]

Survivors were killed on sight. Groups of them were coaxed out of hiding with promises of food and fair treatment, then massacred. Twelve Spaniards were hung in a Catholic church, "dangling from the iron grates within the church windows," an eyewitness reported.[27] Whatever their justification, the killing of prisoners was nothing for the English to brag about. Had an enemy done the same to their men, they would have called it by its right name: murder.

The remnants of the Armada limped into ports along Spain's northern coast. *San Martín* anchored at Santander on September 23, manned literally by a skeleton crew. Half her crew was dead: forty in battle, 180 of sickness. The survivors were bags of bones. For most of the return voyage, Medina Sidonia lay seasick in his bunk with a burning fever, slipping in an out of consciousness. He was so weak that he had to be lowered into a boat to be rowed ashore.

Two days later, he wrote the king's secretary asking to be relieved of his duties. He was through with the sea, he said; all he wanted was to be left in peace. "His Majesty has no need to be served as I have done, with no kind of advantage whatsoever to his cause because I know nothing of the sea nor of war. . . . I hope that he will only want to be done with me. . . . As for affairs of the sea, in no instance and in no way will I ever have anything to do with them again, even if it cost me my head."[28] Philip let him go.

Knowing that he would be blamed for the disaster, Medina Sidonia tried to avoid towns along the way to his home near Cadiz. He traveled in a coach with the curtains drawn, but somehow people learned his identity. Crowds gathered along the way, calling "hey, coward" and throwing stones. In one place, boys chanted, "Drake is coming! Drake is coming!"

Nothing was ready for the crippled fleet. There was no food, no clothing, no hospitals, no medical supplies. An official report stated that ships' crews were "dying like bugs." Here, at least, was a situation the king could handle. Unlike Elizabeth, he spared no effort in aiding the needy. Within days, supplies were on their way to the seaports. Thanks to Philip's personal intervention, hundreds of lives, possibly thousands, were saved.

Spain went into mourning. Of the Armada's 130 vessels, exactly half returned—and of these, perhaps twenty-five were so badly damaged they had to be scrapped. There were villages in which every family lost a loved one, or knew someone who had. Of the 30,000 men

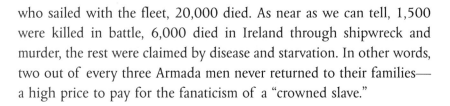

who sailed with the fleet, 20,000 died. As near as we can tell, 1,500 were killed in battle, 6,000 died in Ireland through shipwreck and murder, the rest were claimed by disease and starvation. In other words, two out of every three Armada men never returned to their families—a high price to pay for the fanaticism of a "crowned slave."

CHAPTER VI

End of the Voyage

*The waves became his winding sheet, the waters
    were his tomb
But for his fame the ocean sea was not sufficient
    room.*

                    —ANONYMOUS, 1597

On Sunday, November 24, 1588, the bells of London's St. Paul's Cathedral rang out in joyous thanksgiving. Surrounded by the gentlemen of her court, Queen Elizabeth rode through the city in a golden chariot drawn by white horses. Halting at the cathedral's West Door, she stepped down, knelt in the entryway, and gave thanks for God's mercy toward herself and the English nation. As she rose to go inside, a choir sang words she had written for the occasion:

> *He made the winds and waters rise
> To scatter all my enemies.*

We do not know if Sir Francis Drake was at St. Paul's that day. If he was, he would have agreed with Her Majesty's words—only with a slight addition: God had indeed given England victory, but he, Drake, was the instrument of victory, the Sword of the Lord.

Drake had never been so warmly praised by his countrymen, nor felt so good about himself. At the height of his fame, he looked to the future with unbounded assurance. And why not? For twenty years, whatever he touched had turned to gold. Like other famous people, he had developed a "habit of success," a self-confidence based upon solid achievement. Nothing seemed beyond his ability. There was nothing he could not do once he set his mind to it.

DON ANTONIO DE CRATO CLAIMED THE THRONE OF PORTUGAL, PROMISING TO ALLY HIMSELF WITH THE ENGLISH IF THEY HELPED HIM DRIVE OUT THE SPANISH INVADERS.

Yet things were not as they seemed. Although no one could have known it at the time, Drake's glory days were over. The Armada year was to be his last good one. From then on, his luck would desert him, and failure follow failure.

By a strange quirk of fate, his first failure grew out of his latest success. The Armada had been defeated, not destroyed. Its ships, scattered among Spain's northern ports, were in no condition to fight—at least for a while. But within a year, they could be repaired and crews found for another Enterprise of England. Drake, who did not like to leave a job half-done, hoped to finish them off before they became a threat.

He also wanted to start a fire in King Philip's back yard. Don Antonio de Crato, a Portuguese prince who claimed the throne, had fled to England after the Spanish invasion. An exile living on others' charity, he would have done anything, said anything, to gain the throne. He boasted that the people would rebel the moment he returned with an English army at his back. Success would bring large rewards to England: a military alliance with a grateful Portugal and trading rights in its colonies. Better still, England would get an island in the Azores from which to attack Spanish treasure fleets returning from the New World.

Drake believed these actions would cripple Spain as a world power. Queen Elizabeth had her doubts, particularly about Portugal, but was willing to give her "deare pyrat" a chance. As usual, a company was formed in which the partners contributed ships and money in return for a share of the booty; the "private sector" had to lend a hand, since the government could not afford to mount a large expedition. Her Majesty lent six Royal Navy ships, including the *Revenge*, which Drake again chose as his flagship. Altogether, he commanded eighty ships and over 23,000 men, of whom 15,000 were soldiers under that old warhorse Sir John ("Black Jack") Norreys. In effect, Drake would be leading an "English Armada."

The aims of the expedition were set down in written instructions from the queen. First, it must destroy the remnants of the Spanish fleet. This meant an attack on Santander, where forty of the largest ships were under repair, and San Sebastian, another key port. Second, it was to capture Lisbon for Don Antonio. Finally, it must set up a permanent base in the Azores. The instructions were silent on another point, which everyone took for granted: Drake was to bring home as much booty as possible. A tall order, to be sure—but Sir Francis had always come through.

Things got off to a bad start—and kept getting worse. The weather refused to cooperate. For two weeks, contrary winds kept the fleet bottled up in Plymouth harbor, using up the provisions stored on board. When it finally sailed on April 18, 1589, supplies were running dangerously low and men were falling ill. Also, the queen had promised heavy cannons for siege operations ashore, but these never arrived.

Drake disobeyed orders. Instead of going to Santander, he headed for Corunna. To this day, no one can explain why. The best guess is that one of Don Antonio's followers, a Spanish spy, gave him false reports that many ships had recently put into Corunna. When the English arrived, however, they found one vessel, a galleon, which the captain burnt rather than let it fall into their hands. *El Draque* then set out to loot the city and destroy everything of military value.

Corunna was actually two cities: a lower business and residential section adjoining a "high town," or fortress built on a hilltop. Black Jack's men easily broke through the defenses of the lower city. Fearing the worst, citizens fled before them in panic. History repeated itself; as at Cadiz, people were crushed in the narrow streets leading to the fortress. Unlike Cadiz, however, the English contributed to the loss of innocent lives. Following closely behind the fleeing Spaniards, they cut down about five hundred civilians with swords and pikes. "Glad was the Englishman that could kill one," a soldier boasted.[1]

It would have been worse had they not found more interesting things to do. Wine shops were located throughout the lower city, a temptation few could resist. Passing soldiers rolled the huge barrels into the streets, bashed in their tops, and drank from cupped hands. The effect of strong wine on empty stomachs made them roaring drunk. Comrades stopped to join them and, before long, men lay in the gutters, blocking the way. Hundreds of soldiers were permanently drunk during their stay in Corunna. This, coupled with eating large quantities of raw fruit, made entire units unfit for duty.

Lacking heavy guns, Drake had to haul ships' culverins into position to bombard the fortress. But it was useless; their light balls could not penetrate the thick stone walls. Corunna's defenders were equally strong, beating off one charge after another. None was braver than María Pita, who had seen her army officer husband killed during an attack. Grabbing a sword and shield, María stood shoulder to shoulder with the Spanish troops. Her courage was contagious, and soon hundreds of civilians had joined the battle. The king later gave María an army officer's pension for life.

Drake decided to call it quits after two weeks. All he had to show for his efforts was some food taken from local warehouses and a few captured cannons. Still, he put on a bold front. "We have done the King of Spain many pretty services in this place," he wrote Walsingham, "and yet I believe he will not thank us."[2]

Lisbon was next. On May 16, Norreys led nine thousand men ashore at Peniche, a coastal town forty miles north of the Portuguese capital. The plan was almost an exact copy of Drake's previous attacks on Santo Domingo and Cartagena. While the troops marched overland, the fleet would sail up the Tagus River and strike from the south. It would hold the defenders' attention, allowing Norreys to break in from the rear.

Lisbon had a small Spanish garrison, which the people despised. No doubt they would have rebelled had Drake promptly entered the city with Don Antonio. Unfortunately, Drake met his match in the governor, Albert of Austria, who was King Philip's nephew as well as a cardinal in the Roman Catholic church and an army general.

What Albert lacked in manpower, he made up for in ruthlessness and willpower. Upon learning that the English were at Corunna, he rounded up suspected troublemakers. He was not interested in legal niceties or trials. Albert became judge, jury, and executioner rolled into one. Some he beheaded, others he jailed, and still others he sent to

Spain in chains. The executions took place in public, as a warning to would-be rebels. By this "timely terrorism," he so frightened the people that only a handful rallied to Don Antonio.

Norreys needed five days for the march to Lisbon. There was no serious opposition; the small Spanish units sent to stop him were easily pushed aside. Even so, he lost an average of four hundred men a day. Typhus had reared its ugly head once again. The general had also counted on the peasants to feed his men, but they dared not help. By the time he reached Lisbon, two thousand were dead. Having lost the element of surprise, and lacking artillery, he had to retreat.

Drake, meanwhile, was going nowhere fast. He did manage to land some troops to capture Cascaes, a fishing port at the mouth of the Tagus. And there he stayed. The approaches to Lisbon were just as strong as he remembered them. Rather than risk the fleet, he called meetings to discuss the situation. Meeting followed meeting, day followed day, until the need to make a decision had passed. Norreys reached Cascaes and the fleet put to sea.

Typhus was now racing through the ships. If anything was to be accomplished, it had to be soon. After burning Vigo for the second time, Drake headed for the Azores, only to run into a storm that nearly sank the *Revenge*. The game was over.

He reached Plymouth in mid-June, barely ten weeks after setting out. Casualty estimates range between eleven and seventeen thousand dead, not of wounds, but of disease. The survivors were discharged hungry and in rags. As volunteers, they earned no wages but were to share in the loot; since there was no loot, they were penniless. Some formed gangs to rob travelers along the roads; others rioted in London. It was a dismal end to an ambitious project.

*C*harges were brought against Drake and Norreys for disobeying orders. They defended themselves, claiming bad weather had made it impossible to attack Santander. The case never went to trial and no action was taken against them. Nevertheless, Her Majesty found it easier to forgive the soldier than the sailor. In 1590, she sent Norreys to aid the French Protestants. Drake's disgrace lasted six years.

Losing the queen's favor must have hurt Drake deeply, but he never spoke of it for the record. He certainly didn't sulk. Returning to

Plymouth, he took up his duties as mayor. Besides modernizing its defenses, paying much of the cost himself, he built flour mills to provide the fleets with biscuit and had fresh water piped into the town. As a member of Parliament, he sat on various committees, notably one on the welfare of seamen. When things moved too slowly, he and Hawkins established the Chatham Chest, England's first pension plan. This was an iron box with a hole in the lid through which sailors put a few pennies each month to help the sick and wounded. Until then, a crippled sailor could only hope to be taken back to his hometown, which was supposed to care for him. If he was lucky, he received a license to beg. If not, he starved.

The war dragged on. Drake and Hawkins wanted to post naval squadrons off the Spanish coast to cut off the treasure fleets, but Queen Elizabeth would not listen; she had lost confidence in seamen. Most of the Royal Navy was laid up in dockyards and its expenses cut to the bone.

The years after the Armada were the heyday of the privateer. Vessels swarmed out of ports along the channel coast in search of Spanish prizes. The majority returned empty-handed, or captured small prizes, but there were always a few who struck it rich. The luckiest was George Clifford, Earl of Cumberland. In 1592, he captured the two-thousand-ton *Madre de Dios* (*Mother of God*), the largest ship afloat. She carried a fabulous cargo of spices, silks, carpets, drugs, ivory carvings, and jewels. Instead of turning in the loot right away, Cumberland's men stole as much as they could lay their hands on. One fellow kept eighteen hundred diamonds and between two and three hundred rubies; another took a box with half a peck (four quarts) of pearls. The remainder, possibly half the cargo, was worth £150,000, an all-time record for a prize. Her Majesty profited most of all, earning £90,000 on an investment of £3,000. Cumberland's share was £36,000, more than twice as much as Drake had ever made on a voyage.

King Philip had thought deeply about the Armada's defeat. Nothing could shake his belief that his cause was God's. Given this "truth," everything else followed logically—at least to his mind. If God allowed the disaster, then it must have been because His servant, Philip, had sinned. The king convinced himself that his sins were self-delusion and ignorance. He had fooled himself into believing that God would send miracles to cover his mistakes. Everyone knows God helps those who help themselves. Yet he had not helped himself enough. He had not studied the facts carefully enough or prepared the Enterprise of England well enough. By mending his ways, surely, next time, God would give him victory.

More letters flowed from the Escorial. Slowly, carefully, the Spanish navy was rebuilt and modernized. Dockyards turned out galleons modeled upon Hawkins's ships. Long-range culverins and better trained gunners made them more dangerous than the old "castled" ships. In the New World, defenses at key ports like Cartagena and San Juan de Puerto Rico were strengthened. Small ships called *avisos* (advices) carried news and orders across the Atlantic in twenty-eight days, top speed by sixteenth-century standards. The clumsy treasure fleets were replaced by a more efficient system. Treasure was unloaded at Havana and transferred to a new type of vessel for the voyage to Spain. Known as the frigate, this vessel was fast enough to make it across the ocean without escorts and carried enough guns to shoot its way out of most tight spots. The frigate would eventually become a deadly warship in its own right. In the early years of the republic, the United States Navy was built around frigates like the *Constitution* and *Constellation*. Today's frigates carry rapid-fire cannons and ship-to-ship missiles.

Early in 1595, Drake made another daring proposal. The Spanish recovery, he said, would continue so long as the treasure flowed. Instead of picking off individual vessels, England should go to the source. And, as ever, Panama was the key. He offered to land an army at Nombre de Dios, march across the Isthmus, and capture Panama City. Once in English hands, the city would be turned into a fortress and a naval base. Using it as a strongpoint, English vessels, built in Panama, could seize treasure ships the moment they left Peru.

The Royal Council debated his proposal for months without reaching a decision. It was the Spaniards themselves who forced the issue. In July, King Philip tested his new-found strength with raids on England's southwestern coast. A fleet of forty ships attacked without warning. Several villages—Mousehole, Newlyn, St. Paul—were burned. Penzance, a large town sixty miles west of Plymouth, was treated as *El Draque* had treated many a Spanish town. The raids came just as it was learned that a crippled galleon, carrying two-and-a-half million ducats worth of gold and silver, had been forced into San Juan de Puerto Rico by a storm.

Queen Elizabeth called Drake out of retirement. He and Hawkins were to return to their old stomping grounds in the Caribbean with twenty-seven ships, including six royal vessels. The fleet would have twenty-five hundred men, of whom a thousand were soldiers led by Sir Thomas Baskerville, a veteran of the wars in the Low Countries.

Drake's name still held its magic. No sooner was it announced that he was fitting out an expedition, than volunteers swarmed into Plymouth. The enemy was equally impressed. When the news reached Spain, nine thousand soldiers deserted their units rather than be around if Drake raided the seacoast towns where they were stationed. Churches filled to overflowing, and priests prayed fervently for divine protection. At Lisbon, civilians fled into the surrounding countryside. *El Draque* was coming!

On August 29, the fleet sailed from Plymouth. Actually, it was two fleets: one led by Drake on the *Defiance*, the other by Hawkins on the *Garland*. This arrangement violated the basic military principle of unity of command, the idea that one person should make the decisions and take the responsibility for whatever happened. Why the queen decided to have two admirals is a mystery. Whatever her reason, it was wrong.

An infantry officer named Captain Thomas Maynarde knew the cousins well. He described Hawkins as "a man old and wary, entering into matters with so leaden a foot that the other's meat would be eaten before his spit could come to the fire."[3] Hawkins was sixty-three, considered a ripe old age in those days. He was also tired, sick, and worried; just before sailing, he learned that his son Richard had been captured by the Spaniards. Drake was at least fifty, no youngster either.

Each man was set in his ways and wanted to have his way all the time. After a few weeks at sea, Maynarde wrote, "the fire in their stomachs began to break forth." They argued about everything. One argument grew so hot that they would have gone at each other with swords had Baskerville not stepped between them. Hawkins wanted to go directly to Puerto Rico, while there was still a chance of catching the enemy by surprise. Drake, however, insisted upon attacking the Canary Islands to replenish his supplies. Hawkins gave in; it was against his better judgment, but he felt he had no choice. Had he held firm, he might well have taken the treasure ship.

The attack on the Canaries failed miserably. Several Englishmen were killed and one of the landing parties captured. The expedition's destination had been a closely guarded secret. One of the prisoners, however, had overheard Hawkins mention it to an officer. After some hard-fisted persuasion, he revealed everything to the Spaniards. Next day, an *aviso* sailed for San Juan de Puerto Rico. The governor had the treasure taken ashore and relayed the warning throughout the Spanish Main.

The English appeared on November 12, only to find the city ready and waiting. Shore batteries opened fire at once. One shot toppled *Defiance's* mizzenmast, another crashed into Drake's cabin. He had just sat down to drink a cup of beer when the ball knocked the chair out from under him. It went on to kill two officers, splashing the cabin walls with their blood and brains.

The fleet had already suffered a severe loss. Hawkins had come down with dysentery while crossing the Atlantic and was dying by the time they reached San Juan de Puerto Rico. As the ships took up their positions, he dictated an addition to his will. In it, he left the queen £2,000 "to make your Majesty the best amends" for money she would lose by the failure of the expedition.[4] He passed away before the Spanish guns opened fire.

Drake probed the city's defenses for two days, only to be driven off with heavy losses. For the second time, he had to retreat in the face of a determined enemy. His men were discouraged; they had expected only victory in his service. To raise their spirits, and his own, he made them a promise: "I will bring you to twenty places far more wealthy and easier to be gotten."[5] It was a promise he could not keep.

Drake sailed for the Spanish Main. There he had made his reputation, and there he expected fresh triumphs. Cartagena, however, was stronger than when he had taken it ten years earlier, and he turned away without firing a shot. A few coastal towns were taken and burned, but there was little booty. Warned of his approach, the inhabitants had fled into the forest with their valuables.

On December 27, two days after Christmas, he captured Nombre de Dios. He had come full circle. As a young man, he had broken into the Treasure House of the World with a small band of adventurers. Now he was back at the head of a powerful fleet. But it was different. *Everything* was different. The streets were empty, the markets deserted, and most of the houses empty. The mule trains no longer arrived there from Panama City. Now they went to Porto Bello, a new town several miles to the north. Having lost its reason to exist, Nombre de Dios was dying as a community.

If the mule trains no longer came, their old trail still existed. Long ago, Drake had made his fortune along that very trail. Once again, he vowed, it would be his highway to Panama City.

The Cimaroon could have told him differently, except they were nowhere to be seen. King Philip had never forgotten their role in Drake's raid. To prevent further raids, he ordered them wiped off the face of the earth. Spanish troops mounted several all-out drives, burning Cimaroon villages and driving the survivors deeper into the jungle. They were so cowed that they dared not lift a finger against Spain.

On December 29, Basker-ville set out with eight hundred picked men. It was rough going—the roughest march, soldiers claimed, Englishmen had ever made. But instead of ambushing the enemy, as Drake had done, they themselves were ambushed and forced to retreat. Three days later, they staggered into Nombre de Dios, vowing never to set foot in the jungle again.

Drake was stunned by the setback. His mood changed, so much so that his men hardly recognized him. He seemed to age overnight, becoming jittery, even fearful. "Since our return from Panama he never carried mirth nor joy in his face," Maynarde reported.[6]

The fleet sailed toward Honduras and Nicaragua, where there were supposed to be rich towns ripe for looting. Nombre de Dios was left behind in flames.

Contrary winds forced the fleet to anchor off an island ninety miles west of Porto Bello. Dysentery had become an epidemic and Drake took to his bed. He lay in his cabin, growing weaker by the day.

Disease ravaged his body, but the worst torment was in his mind. He had learned about the New World as a youngster, only to find that the world he knew had vanished in his old age. "He answered me with grief," Maynarde recalled, "protesting . . . that he never thought any place could be so changed, as it were from a delicious and pleasant arbor to a waste and desert wilderness."[7]

Gold! Gold! Day and night it filled his thoughts. It meant more to him than material wealth; he was a rich man and needed nothing that money could buy. Gold had become the measure of his success and the certainty that God favored him. "God hath many things in store for us," he moaned, "and I know many means to do Her Majesty good service and to make us rich, for we must have gold before we see England."[8] He would sooner die than return without the metal.

Baskerville took the fleet back to Porto Bello. It was Drake's last voyage. In the early hours of January 28, 1596, he became delirious and raved like a lunatic. His strength failing, he crawled from his bed and put on his armor, saying he wished to die like a soldier. A servant helped him dress, then put him back to bed. He died quietly at four o'clock in the morning.

They buried him like a Viking chief. Like other sea captains, he had sailed with his own coffin stowed in the ship's hold. It was made of lead. Four of the smaller ships, no longer needed by the fleet, were anchored in a circle around the *Defiance*. Trumpets sounded a mournful tune. Drake's drum, which he had used to signal so many attacks, gave the final salute. Then, while all the guns in the fleet roared, the coffin was lowered into the sea. As it disappeared from view, the four ships, together with Porto Bello, burst into flame. The coffin is still there, resting on the bottom a few miles from the eastern entrance of the Panama Canal.

*E*ngland mourned its lost hero. Spaniards celebrated. He was still *El Draque* to them, the Dragon who killed Spanish men, stole Spanish treasure, and burned Spanish cities. In Madrid, a festival was held in honor of his passing. Lope de Vega wrote a poem, *La Dragontea*, portraying him as a demon in human form. Philip II felt twenty years younger, if only for a few days. Already a dying man himself, he perked up when the word came. "It is good news, and now I will get well," he told visitors.[9]

Drake or no Drake, the war continued. In June, 1596, Lord Howard captured Cadiz and looted it for sixteen days. When he left, it was set on fire and much of it destroyed, including a magnificent cathedral dating from the Middle Ages. Philip launched three more armadas, in 1596, 1597, and 1598. They were driven back not by English ships, but by foul weather. His Majesty never understood why God denied him victory.

Neither Philip nor Elizabeth lived to see the end of the war. Philip died soon after the fourth armada. He was in constant pain during his last months, his body a mass of open sores. "Look at me," he told his son, the future Philip III. "This is what the world and all kingdoms amount to in the end."[10] The English queen died in 1603 at the age of seventy. The Treaty of London brought peace the following year.

*The worlds furuaied bounds, braue **Drake** on thee did gaze,*
Both North and Southerne Poles, haue feene thy manly face.
If thankleffe men conceale, thy prayfe the ftarres woulde blaze,
The Sunne his fellow-trauellers worth will duely grace
Ro. Vaughan fculp.

Drake was gone but not forgotten. Calling themselves "buccaneers," the privateers of the 1600s were his true descendants. These men took courage from his example, while trying to outdo him in every way. Henry Morgan, "the buccaneer prince," succeeded in one respect. In 1671, Morgan led fourteen hundred men across the Isthmus of Panama. The great prize, Panama City, was destroyed. The loot was so great that a hundred seventy-five mules were needed to carry it away. Like Drake, Morgan received a knighthood for his exploits against the Spaniards.

Drake's memory lives on. Buckland Abbey, his home, is today the Drake Museum, a popular tourist attraction. There one can see the drum, his best-known relic. Legend has it that he made a solemn promise while on his deathbed. If ever England was in danger, the sound of that drum would bring him back from the grave.

In 1896, Sir Henry Newbolt turned the legend into a poem. Toward the end, he has Drake say:

> *Take my drum to England, hang it by the shore,*
> *Strike it when your powder's runnin' low;*
> *If the Dons sight Devon, I'll quit the port of Heaven,*
> *An' drum them up the Channel as we drummed them long ago.*

"As we drummed them long ago" is another way of saying, "We did it before, and we will do it again." It is a good attitude to have when the chips are down.

They were certainly down in 1940 and 1941. During the early stages of World War II, the armies of Adolf Hitler massed across the channel for another enterprise of England. There are still those who remember what it was like to patrol the beaches on foggy nights. They will look you straight in the eye and tell of hearing a sound "out there," over the water. It was an unearthly throbbing, the steady rap, rap, rap of a spirit drum.

Thus, Drake's legend became greater than the man himself. In it he lives on as a symbol of courage and persistence, a symbol for people to rally around in times of danger.

Some More Books

There are many books on Sir Francis Drake and his times. I found these the most useful.

Andrews, Kenneth R. *Drake's Voyages: A Reassessment of Their Place in Elizabethan Maritime Expansion.* New York: Scribner's, 1967.

Benson, E. F. *Sir Francis Drake.* London: John Lane, 1927.

Bradford, Ernle. *Drake.* New York: Dorset, 1991.

Corbett, Sir Julian S. *Drake and the Tudor Navy; with a history of the rise of England as a maritime power.* 2 volumes, New York: Burt Franklin, 1966. Reprint of a book first published in London in 1898. This is still the standard biography of Drake, the one authors usually consult first.

————. *Sir Francis Drake.* Westport, Conn.: Greenwood Press, 1970. Reprint of a book first published in 1890.

Drake, Sir Francis. *Francis Drake Revived.* London, 1626. A book by Drake's nephew and heir. In Hampden.

Fernandez-Armesto, Felipe. *The Spanish Armada: The Experience of War in 1588.* New York: Oxford University Press, 1989.

Graham, Winston. *The Spanish Armadas.* Garden City, N.Y.: Doubleday & Co., 1972. The Story of the Four Enterprises of England.

Grierson, Edward. *King of Two Worlds: Philip II of Spain.* New York: G. P. Putnam's Sons, 1974.

Hakluyt, Richard. *Voyages & Documents.* London: Oxford University Press, 1958.

Hampden, John, ed. *Francis Drake, Privateer: Contemporary Narratives and Documents.* London: Eyre Methuen, 1972.

Hardy, Evelyn. *Survivors of the Armada.* London: Constable, 1966.

Hart-Davis, Duff. *Armada.* New York: Bantam Press, 1988.

Hibbert, Christopher. *The Virgin Queen: Elizabeth I, Genius of the Golden Age.* New York: Addison-Wesley, 1991.

Howarth, David. *The Voyage of the Armada: The Spanish Story.* New York: Penguin Books, 1981.

Kemp, Peter. *The British Sailor: A Social History of the Lower Deck.* London: J. M. Dent, 1970.

Kenny, Robert W. *Elizabeth's Admiral: The Political Career of Charles Howard.* Baltimore: Johns Hopkins Press, 1970.

Las Casas, Bartholomé. *The Devastation of the Indies: A Brief Account.* Baltimore: Johns Hopkins University Press, 1992.

Lewis, Michael. *The Spanish Armada.* New York: Crowell, 1966.

Littleton, Taylor D. and Robert R. Rea. *The Spanish Armada.* New York: American Book Company, 1964.

Lloyd, Christopher. *The British Seaman, 1200–1860: A Social Survey.* Rutherford, N.J.: Fairleigh Dickenson University Press, 1976.

———. *Sir Francis Drake.* London: Faber & Faber, 1957.

McFee, William. *The Life of Sir Martin Frabisher.* New York: Harper and Brothers, 1928.

McKee, Alexander. *From Merciless Invaders: An Eye-witness Account of the Spanish Armada.* New York: W. W. Norton, 1964.

———. *The Queen's Corsair: Drake's Journey of Circumnavigation, 1577–1580.* London: Souvenir Press, 1978.

Mannix, Daniel P. *Black Cargoes: A History of the Atlantic Slave Trade, 1518–1865.* London: Longmans, 1962.

Mason, A. E. W. *The Life of Francis Drake.* London: Hodder & Stoughton, 1950.

Mattingly, Garrett. *The Armada.* Boston: Houghton Mifflin, 1959.

Nuttall, Zilia, ed. *New Light on Drake: A Collection of Documents Relating to His Voyage of Circumnavigation, 1577–1580.* London: Hakluyt Society, Second Series, No. XXXIV, 1914. A basic source book.

Padfield, Peter. *Armada: A Celebration of the Four Hundredth Anniversary of the Defeat of the Spanish Armada, 1588–1988.* Washington, D.C.: Naval Institute Press, 1988.

———. *Guns at Sea.* London: Hugh Evelyn, 1973.

Parker, Geoffrey. *Philip II.* Boston: Little, Brown, 1978.

Peterson, Mendel. *The Funnel of Gold*. Boston: Little, Brown, 1975. A fascinating history of the Spanish treasure fleets from the earliest times until the early 1700s.

Pierson, Peter. *Commander of the Armada: The Seventh Duke of Medina Sidonia*. New Haven: Yale University Press, 1989.

———. *Philip II*. London: Thames & Hudson, 1975.

Pringle, Roger, ed. *A Portrait of Elizabeth I in the Words of the Queen and Her Contemporaries*. Totowa, N.J.: Barnes & Noble, 1980.

Robinson, Gregory. *Elizabethan Ship*. London: Longman, 1973.

Roche, T. W. E. *The Golden Hind*. New York: Praeger, 1973.

Sale, Kirkpatrick. *The Conquest of Paradise: Christopher Columbus and the Columbian Legacy*. New York: Plume, 1991.

Sugden, Roger. *Sir Francis Drake*. New York: Touchstone, 1992.

Thomson, George M. *Sir Francis Drake*. London: Secker & Warburg, 1972.

Thrower, Norman J. W., ed. *Francis Drake and the Famous Voyage, 1577–1580: Essays Commemorating the Quadricentennial of Drake's Circumnavigation of the Earth*. Berkeley and Los Angeles: University of California Press, 1984.

Unwin, Rayner. *The Defeat of John Hawkins: A Biography of His Third Slaving Voyage*. New York: Macmillan, 1960.

Whiting, Roger. *The Enterprise of England: The Spanish Armada*. New York: St. Martin's Press, 1988.

Williams, Neville. *Francis Drake*. London: Weidenfeld & Nicolson, 1973.

———. *The Sea Dogs: Privateers, Plunder and Piracy in the Elizabethan Age*. New York: Macmillan, 1975.

Williamson, James A. *The Age of Drake*. London: Adam & Charles Black, 1960.

———. *Hawkins of Plymouth*. New York: Barnes & Noble, 1969.

———. *Sir Francis Drake*. Hampden, Conn.: Archon Books, 1966.

Wilson, Derek. *The World Encompassed: Francis Drake and His Great Voyage*. New York: Harper & Row, 1977.

Notes

CHAPTER I

1. Kenneth R. Andrews, *Drake's Voyages: A Reassessment of Their Place in Elizabethan Maritime Expansion* (New York: Scribner's, 1967), 23.

2. Quoted in Alexander McKee, *The Queen's Corsair: Drake's Journey of Circumnavigation, 1577–1580* (London: Souvenir Press, 1978), 214.

3. Bartholomé de las Casas, *The Devastation of the Indies: A Brief Account* (Baltimore: Johns Hopkins University Press, 1992), 127–128.

4. John Hampden, ed., *Francis Drake, Privateer: Contemporary Narratives and Documents* (London: Eyre Methuen, 1972), 32.

5. A ship's tonnage was based not on its weight, but on the size of its cargo hold. A ton, or tun, was a barrel that contained 252 gallons of wine. Therefore, the hold of a 300-ton ship had space for 300 such barrels.

6. Quoted in Gregory Robinson, *Elizabethan Ship* (London: Longmans, 1973), 10.

7. Quoted in Peter Kemp, *The British Sailor: A Social History of the Lower Deck* (London: J. M. Dent, 1970), 2.

8. *Ibid.*, p. 13.

9. Quoted in Christopher Lloyd, *The British Seaman, 1200–1860: A Social Survey* (Rutherford, N.J.: Fairleigh Dickinson University Press, 1976), 33.

10. Quoted in E. F. Benson, *Sir Francis Drake* (London: John Lane, 1927), 19.

11. Rayner Unwin, *The Defeat of John Hawkins: A Biography of His Third Slaving Voyage* (New York: Macmillan, 1960), 94.

12. Ibid., p. 95.

13. Job Hortop, *The Travailes of Job Hortop,* in Richard Hakluyt, *Voyages & Documents* (London: Oxford University Press, 1958), 117.

14. Quoted in A. E. W. Mason, *The Life of Francis Drake* (London: Hodder & Stoughton, 1950), 14.

15. Quoted in Kemp, *The British Sailor*, 18.

16. Hortop, *Travailes*, pp. 118–120.

17. Quoted in J. A. Williamson, *Hawkins of Plymouth* (New York: Barnes & Noble, 1969), 133. A sailing ship had to be weighted down to prevent it from riding too high in the water and tipping over in bad weather. Ballast, as the added weight was called, was usually tons of stones or sand taken from a beach and kept in the ship's lowest hold.

18. Quoted in T. W. E. Roche, *The Golden Hind* (New York: Praeger, 1973), 17.

19. *Ibid.,* p. 18.

20. *Ibid.,* p. 23.

Chapter II

1. The Low Countries included the Dutch-speaking areas that later became the Netherlands; Flanders, or the Flemish-speaking areas, became modern Belgium.

2. Quoted in George Malcolm Thomson, *Sir Francis Drake* (London: Secker & Warburg, 1972), 43.

3. Sir Francis Drake, *Francis Drake Revived* (London,1626), 55. Messages to be left outdoors were always engraved on lead or brass plates; paper would decompose in the first downpour.

4. *Ibid.,* p. 60.

5. Julian S. Corbett, *Sir Francis Drake* (Westport, Conn.: Greenwood Press, 1970), 28.

6. Quoted in Thomson, *Sir Francis Drake*, pp. 70–71.

7. Quoted in John Hampden, ed., *Francis Drake, Privateer: Contemporary Narratives and Documents* (London: Eyre Methuen, 1972), 46–47.

8. In addition to Panama, there were Cimaroon communities in Mexico, Santo Domingo, Cuba, Brazil, and along the Spanish Main.

9. Quoted in Thomson, *Sir Francis Drake*, p. 74.

10. Drake, *Sir Francis Drake Revived*, p. 80.

11. *Ibid.*, p. 83.

12. *Ibid.*, p. 85.

13. *Ibid.*

14. *Ibid.*, p. 88.

15. Quoted in Roger Sugden, *Sir Francis Drake* (New York: Touchstone, 1992), 73.

16. Quoted in Corbett, *Sir Francis Drake*, p. 44.

CHAPTER III

1. Quoted in Duff Hart-Davis, *The Armada* (New York: Bantam Press, 1988), 30.

2. Quoted in Roger Pringle, ed., *A Portrait of Elizabeth I in the Words of the Queen and Her Contemporaries* (Totowa, N.J.: Barnes & Noble, 1980), 76.

3. Quoted in Mason, *Sir Francis Drake*, p. 406.

4. Quoted in James A. Williamson, *Sir Francis Drake* (Hamden, Conn.: Archon Books, 1966), 53.

5. Quoted in Sugden, *Sir Francis Drake*, p. 98.

6. Quoted in Norman J. W. Thrower, ed., *Francis Drake and the Famous Voyage, 1577–1580* (Berkeley and Los Angeles: University of California Press, 1984), 4.

7. Francis Fletcher, *The World Encompassed by Sir Francis Drake.* London: 1628, reprinted in John Hampden, ed., *Francis Drake, Privateer: Contemporary Narratives and Documents* (London: Eyre Methuen, 1972), 136.

8. *Ibid.*, p. 137.

9. *Ibid.*, p. 146.

10. Quoted in Derek Wilson, *The World Encompassed: Francis Drake and His Great Voyage* (New York: Harper & Row, 1977), 89.

11. Quoted in Corbett, *Sir Francis Drake*, p. 75

12. Fletcher, *The World Encompassed*, p. 152.

13. *Ibid.*, p. 143.

14. *Ibid.*, p. 155.

15. *Ibid.*, p. 157.

16. Quoted in Alexander McKee, *The Queen's Corsair*, p. 126.

17. *Ibid.*, p. 127.

18. Quoted in Christopher Lloyd, *Sir Francis Drake* (London: Faber & Faber, 1957), 61.

19. Zilia Nuttall, ed., *New Light on Drake: A Collection of Documents Relating to His Voyage of Circumnavigation, 1577–1580* (London: Hakluyt Society, 1914), 206.

20. *Ibid.*, p. 203.

21. Fletcher, *The World Encompassed*, p. 173.

22. *Ibid.*

23. Quoted in George Masselman, *The Cradle of Colonialism* (New Haven: Yale University Press, 1963), 74.

24. Quoted in Julian S. Corbett, *Drake and the Tudor Navy.* 2 volumes (New York: Burt Franklin, 1966), I: 302.

CHAPTER IV

1. Quoted in John C. Rule, ed., *The Character of Philip II* (Boston: D. C. Heath, 1963), 42.

2. Quoted in Thomson, *Sir Francis Drake*, pp. 154–155.

3. Quoted in Neville Williams, *Sir Francis Drake* (London: Weidenfeld & Nicolson, 1973), 125.

4. Quoted in Sugden, *Sir Francis Drake*, p. 163.

5. Quoted in Thomson, *Sir Francis Drake*, p. 44.

6. Quoted in Peter Pierson, *Philip II* (London: Thames & Hudson, 1975), 43.

7. Quoted in Geoffrey Parker, *Philip II* (Boston: Little, Brown, 1978),100.

8. Quoted in Thomson, *Sir Francis Drake*, p. 181.

9. Quoted in Corbett, *Drake and the Tudor Navy*, II, pp. 40–41.

10. Quoted in Sugden, *Sir Francis Drake*, p. 190.

11. Quoted in Corbett, *Drake and the Tudor Navy*, II, pp. 40–41.

12. Quoted in Kenneth R. Andrews, *Drake's Voyages: A Reassessment of Their Place in Elizabethan Maritime Expansion* (New York: Charles Scribner's Sons, 1967),10.

13. Quoted in Sugden, *Sir Francis Drake*, p. 208.

14. Quoted in Williams, *Sir Francis Drake*, p. 160.

15. Quoted in Garrett Mattingly, *The Armada* (Boston: Houghton Mifflin, 1959), 108.

16. Quoted in Corbett, *Drake and the Tudor Navy*, II, p. 102.

CHAPTER V

1. Quoted in Ernle Bradford, *Drake* (New York: Dorset, 1991), 188.

2. Quoted in David Howarth, *The Voyage of the Armada: The Spanish Story* (New York: Penguin Books, 1981), 46.

3. Quoted in Michael Lewis, *The Armada* (New York: Crowell, 1966), 47. Italics added.

4. Quoted in Peter Pierson, *Commander of the Armada: The Seventh Duke of Medina Sidonia* (New Haven: Yale University Press, 1989), 82.

5. Quoted in Kemp, *The British Sailor*, p. 32.

6. Quoted in Mattingly, *Armada*, p. 216–217. The admiral was not identified, but was probably Juan Martínez de Recalde, Medina Sidonia's second-in-command.

7. *Ibid.*, p. 344.

8. Quoted in Corbett, *Drake and the Tudor Navy*, II, p. 153.

9. Quoted in Howarth, *Voyage of the Armada*, p. 91.

10. Quoted in Parker, *Philip II*, p. 154.

11. Quoted in Hampden, *Francis Drake, Privateer*, p. 250.

12. Quoted in Alexander McKee, *From Merciless Invaders: An Eye-witness Account of the Spanish Armada* (New York: Norton, 1964), 115.

13. Quoted in Howarth, *The Voyage of the Armada*, p. 170.

14. Quoted in Hart-Davis, *Armada*, p. 188.

15. Quoted in Howarth, *The Voyage of the Armada*, p. 173.

16. Quoted in McKee, *From Merciless Invaders*, pp. 107–108.

17. Quoted in Hart-Davis, *Armada*, pp. 196–197.

18. Quoted in McKee, *From Merciless Invaders*, p. 206.

19. *Ibid.*, p. 205.

20. Quoted in Thomson, *Sir Francis Drake*, p. 268.

21. Quoted in Roger Whiting, *The Enterprise of England: The Spanish Armada* (New York: St. Martin's Press, 1988), 143.

22. Quoted in Pringle, *A Portrait of Elizabeth I*, pp. 80–81.

23. Quoted in McKee, *From Merciless Invaders*, p. 233.

24. Quoted in Mason, *Drake*, 405.

25. Quoted in Felipe Fernandez-Armesto, *The Spanish Armada: The Experience of War in 1588* (New York: Oxford University Press, 1989), 210.

26. Quoted in Whiting, *Enterprise of England*, p. 192.

27. Quoted in Hart-Davis, *Armada*, p. 228.

28. Quoted in Pierson, *Commander of the Armada*, p. 171; Fernandez-Armesto, *Spanish Armada*, p. 220.

CHAPTER VI

1. Quoted in Sugden, *Drake*, p. 272.

2. Quoted in Corbett, *Sir Francis Drake*, p. 182.

3. Quoted in Corbett, *Drake and the Tudor Navy*, II, p. 284.

4. Quoted in Mason, *Drake*, pp. 412–413.

5. Quoted in Corbett, *Drake and the Tudor Navy*, II, p. 396.

6. Quoted in Lloyd, *Sir Francis Drake*, p. 177.

7. *Ibid.*, p. 177.

8. *Ibid.*, p. 167.

9. Quoted in Sugden, *Sir Francis Drake*, p. 316.

10. Quoted in Winston Graham, *The Spanish Armadas* (Garden City, N.Y.: 1972), 249.

Index